APACHES AND STEAMBOAT GAMBLERS
Snake and the Dog-Man Book 2

JOHNNY GUNN

WOLFPACK
PUBLISHING
— EST 2018 —

Published in the United States by Wolfpack Publishing, Las
Vegas

Wolfpack Publishing
6032 Wheat Penny Avenue
Las Vegas, NV 89122

wolfpackpublishing.com

Paperback ISBN 978-1-64734-140-4
eBook ISBN 978-1-64734-139-8

APACHES AND
STEAMBOAT GAMBLERS

"Gonna be a long trek to San Simon, Dog. Them pilgrims riding with us gonna give me heart ache for sure." Snake and Dog-man were ten days out of Las Cruces and had spent the previous night at a water hole hosted by the Mimbres Indians. They were guarding two Dawson Freight Company wagons, and two smaller wagons belonging to a family moving to Tucson, Arizona Territory.

Snake, a long, laid-back Texan who seems to just roll along with whatever life offers, enjoying the rain when it fall and the drought when it doesn't. He also has the heart of a poet from time to time and the skill of a trained killer when needed. He doesn't have much use for those who won't take care of themselves.

"The old man ain't got no kind of a sense of humor and the old lady ain't got no sense." Snake thought about what he said for a second or two and had to laugh right out. "Well? Am I wrong?"

"You ain't been wrong a day in your life, Snake. Except for that time back in Deadwood."

"Weren't my fault and you know it," he snuffed. "All right then, we just think about California, more gold, cattle belly deep in sweet grass and not about old man Potter. Won't give Mr. Potter or his often-offended old woman wife another thought."

The boys had struck it rich, totally by accident discovering a mine, probably in Mexico, and were trying to get to California. A dear friend, George Dawson hired them to ride guard on this trip across southern New Mexico and southern Arizona Territory. "Looking forward to Tucson, Dog. Don't know why, but the stories of how the Spanish, two hundred years ago, built the place."

Snake might have had a real name at some point in his thirty-year life, but he never used it. He was long and lean, straight out of the wild lands of west Texas, never sat straight up in the saddle, but rarely got throwed, either. Snake was a hard worker but would scoff at the idea while making up camp and gathering firewood. Snake and Dog-man had been traveling partners for several years.

Dog-man was heavier, strong, but boyish in looks. Flowing blondish hair drew the women, and a fast gun repelled the ugly men. He carried a Henry, that he won in a card game several years before.

"These next few days might get some intense, Dog-man. Keep me away from old man Potter and we'll be fine."

"Dawson said this section from the Mimbres to San Simon is Apache country and they don't much care for us, so Potter might be the least of our worries."

***

Jesse Potter, nearing thirty-years-old, uprooted his family for a new life in in Tucson, Arizona Territory. He couldn't make a farm work in the lush breaks of Missouri, not because of the excellent ground, but because of consumption. His wife Mercy hated the world because of Jesse's illness, believed the world was out to get her.

They had two children, Amos, eight-years-old, and Kenneth, five, neither of whom understood the word no. The family got thrown off one wagon train and old George Dawson felt sorry for them and let them come with the freighters.

"We're moving through Chiricahua country for the next five days or so, Dog-man, but San Simon is right on the San Simon River. Them Pachies are a nasty bunch."

"Each freight wagon has a guard with big guns, Snake, we've got ours, and old man Potter is mean enough to scare a really tough old Apache. Last moving water we seed was the Rio Grande. Hope the San Simon River coming up has a little less mud."

***

The trail was rocky and steep in places, just rocky in others and Snake and Dog-man scouted well out in front of the little train. There were clumps of scrub brush scattered among the rocks and more places to hide men than the Missouri breaks. The plan was to put the two Potter wagons in between the two big freighters, but Mercy Potter, even after some thousand miles of driving her two horses, simply couldn't keep in line.

The problem came to a head at noon break that

day. Earlier, Snake was searching the rocks about a mile in front of the train, sure he had seen a flittering of dust on an airless day. "Keep an eye on me, Dog," he said and rode up the steep hillside toward a scattering of broken rock that had fallen from the towering escarpment the trail skirted.

Dog-man stepped down from his horse, rifle in hand and tucked himself next to a pine tree to watch. Snake dismounted also and moved slowly from tumble of rock to stand of pines, and was about to make another move when Dog-man spotted movement less than fifty yards in front of Snake. "No!" He howled it out.

Snake dropped to the ground, like a rock and saw Dog-man pointing at some rocks off slightly to his left. "Thank you, Dog-man," Snake murmured when he spotted the lone Indian moving about in the rocks, trying to get a bead on where the yelling came from. "Why would you be out here all by yourself watching this old trail?" Talking to himself was a lifelong trait.

Dog-man watched as Snake moved through the rocks to get closer to the lone intruder and took that moment to move himself. *If he ain't alone, Snake's in trouble, and if he is alone, why? We're bringing that bunch of wagons through this little pass in another couple of hours, that's why.*

Dog-man saw Snake looking back toward him and flagged him to come back down. *He's gonna move right into where that fella's brothers are getting ready to strike.*

Snake ignored him and moved through the rocks as quiet as an Indian and spotted the group of Chiricahua braves sitting around a small fire.

"Seven here, one out there some and our wagon train is coming through." He moved back down off the mountain side and found Dog-man.

"I just wanted to see how many, that's all," Snake said. "Ain't no other way around that towering rock than through this pass, Dog-man. With the one up there, there are seven more back in the trees. Gotta bunch them wagons tight coming through."

"Better get back then and get 'em prepared. Might move one of the guards to drive Mrs. Potter's wagon. We gotta go through this pass fast and hard," Dog-man said.

"She won't like that," Snake snickered.

"Not a bit."

2

"Got a nasty, rock strewn pass in front of us and a gathering of locals to keep us from going through. Better hold 'em up, Rhyerson. Need to jaw some." Snake and Dog-man found the lead wagon a mile or so back, along with Jesse Potter's. "Where are the others?"

Ben Rhyerson drove wagons and bossed trains for George Dawson across this foreboding desert for years and was ready to jettison the Potter family. "That woman," he snarled it out. "She couldn't drive a toy horse. Me and Stumpy already had noon meal and they ain't caught up yet. Gotta do something about that, Snake."

"Yes we do. Let's wait 'till they catch up and we'll make some changes. Let's eat something, Dog-man. Might be our last meal."

The two Potter wagons and the other Dawson rig arrived within a half hour and Rhyerson called everyone for a pow-wow. "Moving into the most dangerous part of this here journey of ours and our guides have detected a possible attack. It's time to make some needed changes. What's your plan, Snake?"

"These wagons have to be kept as tight together as possible. Having four wagons spread out over several miles of trail is gonna cost lives. It's obvious that Mrs. Potter shouldn't be driving through this kind of country. I want Sampson Sloan to drive that wagon even though he's supposed to be Hank Thisby's messenger. Can you do that, Sloan?"

"Been driving all my life but that puts Hank in a bad spot."

"Not as bad as being the tail wagon a mile or more behind the lead and the two guides," Hank laughed. "We'll still have your big guns, Sam. I'm all for this change. I don't like being at the end of a train that's in two different territories."

"Well, I'm not," Mercy Potter said. "That's my wagon and I'm driving it. Been driving it since we left Missouri. Plan to drive it into Tucson. Ain't nobody driving them horses but me."

Snake looked over to where Jesse Potter was standing with his two children, waiting for the man to tell his wife that she wouldn't be driving their second wagon. He just stood there, shook his shaggy head of hair a time or two and shrugged his shoulders.

Well, ain't that just like him. Don't give a damn about whether people are gonna die or not as long as he doesn't have to have words with his wife. "Sorry, Mrs. Potter, but that's the way it's gonna be. As long as me and Dog-man are the guides and Ben Rhyerson's the wagon boss, you won't be driving."

Dog-man started to say something but Mercy Potter wasn't through. "Then we ain't in this train."

She stood and walked to where Jesse and the boys were. "We'll do fine alone. Jesse can kill an Indian or two just as good as you, Mr. Snake."

"I think Snake's right, Mercy." Jesse Potter said. "We need to keep these wagons close together and you haven't been doing that. Mr. Sloan said he was a good driver. He'll take good care of the horses."

"I won't stand for it." She screamed right in his face. Kenneth, just five years old started crying, Amos, eight, grabbed his father's pant leg, and Mercy screamed again, "I won't stand for it. That's my wagon to drive. I drive it or it doesn't move and neither do we."

The four Dawson men stood in silence, trying not to look at this woman throwing her temper tantrum, trying not to look at Jesse Potter standing with two frightened children, not saying a word.

"That's enough theatrics," Dog-man said. "Jesse, put your wife and children in your wagon and drive close to Ben Rhyerson. Sloan, drive the other Potter wagon right up behind Jesse and Thisby, drive that heavy wagon of yours hard and fast. Chiricahua Apache Indians are not camp tramps. They are waiting down the trail to kill us all. I'm riding lead, Snake's tailing."

Jesse hustled the kids into his wagon, but Mercy stood like a rock, not even her hair moving in the afternoon wind. "Get in the wagon, Mercy. Time to go."

"No! Not going." She turned from him and walked over to some rocks and sat down.

"This isn't the time, Mercy. Let's go."

Before she could scream out another 'No', Snake walked over, picked her up, despite all the kicking, hitting and screaming and threw her in the back of her wagon. "Move 'em out, Rhyerson," he hollered and walked to his horse. *Dog-man best not ask me again why I don't never want to get hitched up. Be just like that woman to jump out of the wagon when we're fightin' off the 'paches.*

***

"Don't let me get more than thirty or forty feet in front of you, Ben," Dog-man said. "If we go through that pass at a strong trot, we'll have the advantage. They'll come from our right, down a rocky slope. There's a deep ravine, very deep and steep, to our left."

"I'll drive from the left side, then," Ben Rhyerson said. "Stumpy can ride on the right with his rifle, sidearm and shotgun." Stumpy Felton was one of those men that others talked about. One leg was shorter from birth and it took just a year or two at school, facing bullies and he got mean and tough.

Felton almost became an outlaw before meeting up with George Dawson and putting all his anger and muscle into protecting valuable wagons and merchandise. When Felton was on the lead wagon, everyone felt safe.

"You're pretty sure of this attack, aren't you?" Rhyerson asked.

"Yup. Snake almost walked right into the attackers. It weren't no hunting party." He waved back down the line of wagons to Snake, turned his horse and rode off with the lead wagon right behind him. *Maybe ought to give Mrs. Potter a shotgun and tell her it was the Indians decided she couldn't drive her own wagon.*

The trail followed along the edge of the deep ravine and into the narrower pass. The mountains slowly rolled and tumbled in from the right. Dog-man, his eyes never slowing down as he scanned the countryside, put his horse into a trot, hearing the lead wagon picking up speed. The pass continued to narrow, and it was at the point where Snake saw the puff of dust that Dog-man spotted the war party.

He pointed up the mountainside and kicked his horse into a lope as the Indians, still a hundred yards or more up the hill, began to move down. *Why aren't they racing down that hillside, screaming for our blood? Something's wrong.* Dog-man pulled his horse up short, jumped from the saddle, rifle in hand and yelled out.

"We fight from here." All the wagons were jammed together because of the sudden stop and men baled from their seats and saddles to take up positions. The Apaches could only come from the right and the wagon men found rocks, wagon wheels and heavy brush to hide behind.

"Why'd you stop?" Ben Rhyerson was almost angry at this change.

"They aren't coming hard, Ben. There's more of them down the road a piece. Probably just around that big bend down there." Dog-man watched the Indians spread across the side of the hill and move down slowly. He waved and caught everyone's attention.

"They'll be in range shortly and that's when the attack will start. Shoot to kill," he hollered. "Don't just throw a bunch of bullets out there. There's more of them down the road a piece, too."

There were seven well entrenched defenders facing eight apache warriors who knew they had back-up. The Indians were't going to just attack, they were going to slowly eliminate these white men riding through their territory. They moved in groups down the rocky slope, two here, moving fast, two more over there and nobody had fired a shot yet.

"Hold, hold," Dog-man whispered, more to himself than to Ben Rhyerson. Two wildly painted Chiricahua warriors started to move down closer, screaming, their war clubs at the ready. Dog-man had his sights on one of them instantly. The Henry jerked and so did the brave as he tumbled into a sage and fell dead in the rocks. "Now," he whispered again.

It was as if a command had been given to each side. That Chiricahua rose as one and raced toward the wagons. Gunfire echoed through the pass, ugly and frightening screams, too. A warrior, war club swinging, leaped for Ben Rhyerson, but Snake's pistol barked twice, ending the attack. The fight was all over in less than a minute. Four Indians died and four more ran back uphill to plan for the next assault. "Mount up," Dog-man yelled. "Leave these. There are more around the bend."

3

Dog-man rode hard but tried not to pull away from the lead wagon. He needed to be close. Ben Rhyerson was driving the four up hard and the Potter wagons were keeping up. Hank Thisby had the heaviest wagon, pulled by three heavy teams and they were tearing up the road. Snake was following, watching the hillside as much as he could with all the dust flying about.

They were coming to the big bend at one of the narrowest parts of the trail. Great rock pillars and walls towered over the wagons and the gorge on their left seemed hundreds of feet deep. Dog-man picked up his pace and the wagons in turn did, also. They were thundering around the bend and through the narrows when Dog-man spotted a mounted group of Apaches just off the trail, less than fifty yards away. He thought he saw at least ten braves in war paint. *They knew we were coming. Problem with schedules.*

He pointed at them, spurred his horse, and laid out low in the saddle, his handgun ready. He could almost feel the four horses from Rhyerson's wagon breathing down his neck. *Wish I knew what was at the end of this pass. Does it flare out into good rangeland? Is it more steep country filled with rocks? Don't matter, I guess, cuz that's where we're going.*

Shooting from the back of a fast galloping horse wouldn't be anyone's first choice to prove marksmanship, but on the other hand, it makes you an equally difficult target. Dog-man fired at a few of the Indians as they came into his sights and knew he wouldn't hit one but might keep them from shooting back.

Stumpy Felton was sitting high on the freight wagon, his Winchester at his shoulder and was more able to pick a target. The wagon swayed and bumped, but he had fired hundreds of rounds from hard driving wagons and was able to hit at least two members of the Apache war party. Rhyerson had the four up at breakneck speed and wasn't slowing down for anything. "Kill 'em, Stumpy. I ain't slowin' down."

Jesse Potter had his team racing hard to keep up with Rhyuerson, his children screaming in terror in the back. Sloan had the other team at full gallop, Potter's wife screaming in anger at his side. "Shut up, woman and shoot something." He bawled it out and whipped the horses some more. She had an old Spencer and knew how to shoot. At least one Indian went down from her shooting.

Sampson Sloan, in the second Potter wagon, held the reins for the team in one hand and a big Colt in the other. Sitting on the seat next to him was a sawed-off, double barreled ten-gauge shotgun, hammers back. "Come on, you red bastards, I'm ready," he snarled. Two of the raiding party had an angle on Sloan's wagon and he holstered the Colt, grabbed the shotgun, and gave them just enough time to get a bit closer before unleashing the fires of Hades on them.

Thisby wasn't fighting Indians, he was fighting six up through a rock-strewn tight pass while being shot at by the Indians. His salvation came in the form of Snake, riding hard right behind the wagon. Snake's Winchester barked every time one of the red devils made a move on Thisby's wagon.

It was five minutes of incredible danger and the small train made one final bend around a stand of rocky pillars and into a broad, open, miles wide and long mountain meadow. Dog-man spotted a stand of pine trees and directed Rhyerson at them, he rode off to the side to make sure Potter followed, and joined Snake to defend the train while it got settled and the men could make ready for a stand.

The two rode back and forth, Dog-man with his Colt and Henry reloaded and Snake with his fine rifle at the ready, daring the war-party to make their move. They crisscrossed, rode in circles, did anything to keep all the attention on them and not the vulnerable wagons trying to get parked.

"They be comin'," Snake yelled, turning his horse to face six fearsome Chiricahua riding down on them. Dog-man dropped from the saddle, this time with his Henry in hand and fired from a kneeling position, dropping two of the attackers immediately. Before Snake could get a shot off, the others turned and rode off.

"Well, that wasn't very nice," he said. "We're supposed to be partners. You could have let me get one shot off. Now I gotta face those people and they

know I didn't even fire my gun at that bunch." Snake
was in a twit and Dog-man just smiled, mounted up,
and rode back toward the wagons, set up for defense.

"Ain't nobody gonna say nothin', Snake. Let's
make sure we ain't got wounded. I want to talk with
Rhyerson about something, too. The only difference
between what would be a normal Dawson freight
run is us riding as guides. Them 'Paches were waiting for this run. Dawson has these runs on a tight
schedule and these local boys know it."

"That's been his trademark, Dog. You ship with
Dawson, he'll get your shipment there and on time.
You do have a point, though."

They rode into another wild-eyed harangue by
Mrs. Mercy Potter. She was standing with her legs
spread, her fists doubled, screaming into Ben Rhyerson's face. "What is it this time?" Dog-man stepped
down and handed the reins to Snake. "Got a burr
tucked in those skirts?"

"Says her wagon is wrecked and demands that
Dawson Freight pay her for it." Rhyerson spat some
juice into the rocks and started laughing. The laughter got louder and more intense the longer he stood
there looking at the woman. "She's mad, you know,"
and he howled in gales of laughter.

"I'm wondering about you," Snake snickered.
Dog-man took Rhyerson by the arm and led him off
toward a fire one of the teamsters had going. Snake
motioned for Jesse Potter to come over. "We're several days from San Simon, Potter and if your woman
keeps this up, shore as I'm standing right here, one of
these fine upstanding teamsters is gonna shoot her
dead. You get her under control or I will."

"She's just very protective of that wagon and her

horses." Potter stammered some, coughed to try and hide it and never looked at Snake.

"No, Potter," Snake said. "She's plumb crazy. Calm the woman, Potter or I will." He turned and strode toward the fire and some coffee. *Go ahead, Dog-man. I dare you. Ask me when it is, I might want to get hitched.*

***

"We got a lot of daylight left, Ben," Snake said. He poured some whiskey from his flask into the tin-cup of coffee and took a long drink. "Don't want to hang around this area too long. We're at least three days from San Simon and all three might be filled with Apaches. We can't have that woman squallin' the whole time."

"Can't gag and truss her, either," Dog-man said. "Can't whop her across the side of the head every time she opens that yap of hers, either. Potter can't handle her and she don't pay no mind to me or Snake."

Sam Sloan poured some coffee and joined the group. "Those are some fine horses the Potters have. Mizz Potter told me her father bred them on his farm back in Missouri. She seems to think they're fragile for some reason. Hard-headed woman. She's never been properly schooled on driving fine animals. Shame, too, coz them are fine driving animals."

Snake reacted before any of the rest. "That why she wouldn't try to keep up?"

"More'n likely. Just needs to know more about her horses and driving. Her daddy's a breeder of splendid horseflesh, but never taught his daughter a thing about them. All she sees is pretty and that relates to fragile. Them horses could outrun anything we have with us including that charger you ride, Snake."

"Think you could teach her if you continued to ride with her? We still got some mean country to go through."

Snake expected Sloan to take a swing at him, maybe even go for that sidearm of his. Instead, it seemed, he was looking forwards to the idea. "She ain't hard to talk with. Just hard-headed is all. Sure, let her ride with me the rest of today and we'll see."

"Also," Ben Rhyerson said. "If it don't turn out, there's a small farm about a day this side of San Simon and we could just drop the Potters off there. Let's mount up, boys, got daylight left and miles to go."

4

"How do you put any kind of reason to any of it, Snake?" Dog-man and Snake were half a mile or more in front of the Dawson train, enjoying a day without angry Apache Indians or a screaming Mercy Potter.

"Don't be tryin', old man. That woman almost idolizes Sam Sloan right now. Don't rock the boat. We got another full day of peace coming our way if we're lucky, if he can keep her mesmerized with his horse stories, if her husband doesn't get jealous and wreck it for us."

"He weren't too pleased when she had supper with Sloan instead of with her family. Them kids never do quit crying, do they?" Dog-man was watching the open country in front of them, thinking about this job they took on. "Tucson ain't too much past San Simon, Snake. We got full pokes when we get there. I might buy another shirt."

"Ain't nothing wrong with the one you have. You just bought that one a few weeks ago. I'd want to keep right on moving toward California, but I'd also like to spend some time not riding on an endless trail. This ain't been a bad ride," and he had to chuckle right along with Dog-man, "you know, all in all. I'd just like to wake up some morning and not just see more trail spread out in front of me."

Ain't seen country like we did coming down from Denver, but sure have seen flat desert and rocky high mountain desert. There's something missin' on this little trip and I can't put my finger on it. "I don't like towns and cities, Dog, and neither do you. Let's get out and away from Tucson and spend a few days just sittin' in camp thinkin'. We done that before."

"Dust." Dog-man pointed out a plume about three miles out and on the trail. "Get back and warn Rhyerson. I'll keep track of what's coming." Snake was gone that fast and Dog-man rode up on a little rise and stood just under the crest, watching whatever or whoever was approaching.

That little farm Ben Rhyerson was talking about can't be but just a few miles in front of us. Hope that dust is farmer dust and not Chiricahua dust. Looks to be three riders and don't see any other signs of movement.

The wagon train arrived at about the same time as the three riders. "You're running behind schedule, Rhyerson. Ain't like a Dawson train to be late," the lead man yelled out, reining his horse to a dusty stop. "Got people at the farm waitin' for you. George Dawson ain't gonna like my report."

"You can shove that report somewhere dark and damp, Keaton." Rhyerson was glaring at the skinny man. Crabby Pete Keaton owned a small farm with a few head of cattle, some hogs, and a band of sheep. Some of the miners working the high mountains would come down to his farm and catch a ride into Tucson for supplies on a Dawson wagon train coming through.

"Let's keep movin', Ben," Snake said. "I'd allow we're being followed, sneaky busters that they are."

"Who're you, giving orders?" Crabby Pete spun his horse to face Snake.

"Don't matter none who I am, mister. What matters is gettin' this train off this plateau before dark." Snake stood tall in the stirrups and hollered out, "Let's move 'em, boys." He motioned for Dog-man to lead out, nodded to Pete Keaton and nudged his horse into a trot.

"Don't you ride off and not answer me. Just who do you think you're talkin' to? Trail bums don't ignore me, mister."

"That may be," Snake said. "Course I ain't one of them, neither. You got a lot of rudeness built into that skinny little body of yours." Snake rode right up to Crabby Pete's horse and scowled at the man. "My name's Snake. I work for George Dawson. My job is to get this bunch of wagons, freight, and people to Tucson. You're in my way."

He touched the spurs lightly and when his horse stepped out it bumped hard into Keaton's, causing that horse to side-step quickly. Keaton had to grab the saddle horn which brought chuckles from his two companions. Snake paid no mind to anything and loped off to join Dog-man.

Keaton cussed loud, spun his horse and raced to catch up. "You just hold up there, saddle tramp. Nobody talks that way to Pete Keaton. You're gonna answer to that. You're gonna feel the wrath of Pete Keaton, you ignorant bastard."

Snake watched the man make a move for his

sidearm, twisted hard in the saddle and fell to the ground, pulling his heavy Colt free before he hit the ground. He fired just one shot, rolled free of the horses, sprung to his feet, Colt cocked and ready. Crabby Pete Keaton fell from his saddle, too, but it wasn't a controlled fall and there was a lot of blood pouring from his leg.

Snake looked at the two men who had ridden in with Keaton. "Got no fight with you two, but if he's a friend, he needs some help."

"Never called him a friend, but I will help get him patched," one of the men said. "Me and Shaughnessy here were looking for a ride to Tucson. We'll meet you at the ranch. Name's Fairchild."

"Remember what you saw. Don't think he'll tell the same story." The wagons were moving, and Snake rode off to find Dog-man. *What an interesting little meeting that was. To be like that tells me the man don't eat right. I was in favor of leavin' Mizz Potter at that ranch, but I could never be that mean.*

"Hey, Dog." Snake hollered as he rode up. "I had to shoot that fool. Called me a saddle tramp."

"I'd rather be a saddle tramp than an outlaw." Dog-man looked out across the vast openness of desert, craggy mountains and endless sky. "Who are those two riding with him?"

"Said they was waiting for us so's they could ride on into Tucson with us. Didn't stand up for Keaton at all. Man pulled a gun on me, Dog. Rude, that's what he was. Rude."

Dog-man chuckled at the comment. "Ben Rhyerson says we're supposed to spend the night at that farm. Might get a little testy, Snake. Maybe we'll find some trees nearby to camp under."

"Ain't gonna do a job like this again," Snake said. "I know, I know." Snake wasn't gonna let Dog-man lecture him again about why they took the job. "We got to come all this way through hostile Indian country with a bunch of other guns and we're gettin' paid to do it. I know all that, but it changed when Mizz Potter become a part of the program. And now we got Mr. Friendly Keaton to contend with."

"No, sir, Dog, I ain't gonna take another job like this again. Never."

"Well, Snake, when we get to that farm, you can tell me how you really feel. Meantime, let's think about what happens when we get to Tucson."

"I want to see more of this country, Dog. You take the danger of bein' arrowshot out of the picture, it's pretty country. Settle in with good water somewhere, raise some good stock," he let the thought drift off. He stood up in the stirrups and looked all around. "Maybe that's what's missing from this trip. Just you and me talkin'. I like this country. Ain't Texas, mind you, but I like it."

"Man would want a woman with him," Dog-man said. "A woman, bunch of screamin' kids, sweet water, and good stock."

Snake never said a word, just nudged his horse into a gentle lope, but heard the laughter from Dog-man and cussed hard under his breath.

***

"You ain't staying at my farm, you sure as hell ain't eatin' my food." Crabby Pete Keaton was stretched out on a couch, his woman, an Apache, tending the gunshot. "You attacked me and I'm gonna see to it that you pay for that."

"Didn't attack nobody and you know it. Don't want your food and wouldn't sleep in one of your beds anyway." Snake, Dog-man, and Ben Rhyerson were in the living room of Keaton's farmhouse talking with the wounded man about accommodations.

"Them two miners waiting for us said you went for your gun first, Pete," Rhyerson said. "We'll be pulling out at sunrise. Don't be telling lies about our guides and don't be telling me how to boss a freight load. Contract you have with George Dawson is you feed us and bunk us. You're lucky Snake didn't kill you dead. I would have. Let's make camp, boys, I ain't hungry for his food."

Lean-tos were set up near a stand of scrawny pines, good fires were lit, and beans and salt meat were eaten. "This just ain't our kind of work, Dog-man."

"Not sure what our kind of work is, Snake. We're good with cattle. Ain't good with people."

"We were pretty goods miners, Dog. Not worth nothing in a town or city, though." Snake wanted to say more but Sam Sloan walked up and joined them.

"You boys done some ranchin', have you?"

Dog-man nodded, looked at Snake, and motioned for Sloan to sit with them. "Got something on your mind?"

"Working with those horses of Mrs. Potter has brought back some memories. Had an uncle in Nebraska that bred horses and mules and I lived with him for about three years. Learned more about mules than you can imagine. This is mule country. Steep, rocky, narrow. If I find a place between San Simon and Tucson with decent water, I might just settle in. I'll need a couple of good hands."

5

"I liked what old Sloan was talking about," Snake said. "Except for one thing."

"What would that be?" Dog-man poured more whiskey into their cups and grabbed the coffee pot. "You're a natural with horses. Would be with mules, I reason."

"Yup. Helped the army with a load of mules once. Smart. Some say ornery, but I say particular. You say for a mule to do something he don't want to do. He be particular in what he wants to do. You got to entice 'em into wantin' to do something. Can't make 'em do it. They gotta want to." He took a long drink of well-laced hot coffee.

It was a nice evening along a creek running with clean, cool water. The stars were brilliant in a black sky and the day's wind finally gave it up. Tomorrow, back on the trail, but for tonight, it was long conversations about anything and everything.

"Now, about that one thing. There's gonna be trouble before we ever reach San Simon between Sam and old man Potter if he keeps doin' what he's been doin and I don't want to work for a man what busts up a family. There, Dog. I said it."

Snake sat still, staring into the dirt and the fire and the stars, but not at Dog-man. Saying what he said was unusual. Men rarely passed judgement on other men concerning their relationships with women. Women, for the most part, scared the hell out of Snake. He'd dance with one at a saloon, even visit a bawdy house from time to time, but kept his distance from all the others. *For the life of me, I can't imagine living with one. Children? They're fun to watch but not the screamin' kind.* He shook his head, and finally looked up at Dog-man.

"I understand that you might not approve, what with your Victorian upbringing," Dog-man said, not really sarcastically, but close. "Are you serious in thinking he's trying to bust up the marriage?"

"Even if he ain't tryin', it's bustin' up. Jesse Potter's hotter'n a rooster on a chase. Gonna kill Sam, I'm sure. Couldn't work for a man what done that. Couldn't. If I was Potter, I'd just let her go, but then, what to do with them squally kids?"

"Send them right along, too," Dog-man said.

Snake let out a loud laugh and grabbed for the bottle. "Serve him right," Snake laughed some more. "Serve him right."

"Don't mind workin' for somebody," Dog-man said. "We been doing that right along, 'cept for our minin', but I'd rather not if we don't have to."

"We won't never have to Dog. We always forget that we got a poke that's well-filled. We'll figure something out when we get to Tucson. It ain't gonna be with Sloan, though." He let his thoughts drift off. *A man's got to have values that mean something. Mine say that I ain't working for a man whose values are as low as Sloan's.*

***

They had to climb out of the little valley where Keaton's place was early the next morning. The roadway was narrow and rocky, slow going for the heavy freight wagons and Dog-man took the point while Snake rode drag. He held back about a quarter mile from Thisby's heavy wagon and spent most of his time searching the hills and canyons for visitors, letting his mind roam over the previous night's ramblings.

"Sure hope I'm wrong about Sloan," he mumbled. "No man needs to have his woman taken. Mizz Potter needs a good whippin', too." Over about half an hour he took each of the people involved to task and had a satisfied look on his face when he spotted the lone rider high on a hillside.

He rode through the wagons alerting everyone and dashed back to the end of the small train. "One feller in buckskins, but I don't see no paint on him and he don't seem to have company." Snake's eyes searched the mountains all around them and couldn't find any others. He held back some and let the man come down off the hillside and onto the trail.

"I'll be damned. A white man." Snake heard Dog-man ride up behind him, heard the wagons continue on and watched the visitor slowly walk his horse up to them. "About far enough, stranger. You alone?" Snake asked.

"Alone as the day is long," the man said. "You got

Texas in your voice."

"You, too," Snake chuckled. "Ridin' alone out here ain't conducive to good health."

"Folks around here call me Cheyenne and I'm lookin' to keep this hair of mine. Lookin' for a couple of miners. Shaughnessy and Fairchild. Heard they might be headed for Tucson."

"I'm Snake, this here's Dog-man, and those two boys are up in the front wagon. Hope you ain't here to start something. We've had enough of that."

"No trouble from me, but they got trouble." Cheyenne turned his horse and rode up toward the lead wagon.

"I'll ride with you," Dog-man said.

***

"The whole thing, burned to the ground and everything destroyed?" Sean Shaughnessy was almost crying when Cheyenne told him about the Apache raid on their mine. "Everything?"

"Near as I could tell, they weren't a pick still had a handle," Cheyenne said. "Part of Grey Wolf's band, I think. Been raisin' all kinds of trouble around here. Coyote Pete Henderson got hisself killed trying to fight 'em off."

Cheyenne turned to Dog-man. "Might want to add some speed to these buggies and make fast for San Simon. Grey Wolf don't much care for wagons coming through his back yard. I'll ride as far as San Simon if y'awl'll let me."

"Proud to have you along, Cheyenne," Dog-man said. He wheeled his horse to look back down the line of wagons and waved his arms. "Let's move 'em, boys. Lots of daylight left." The road had twists and turns by the dozen, the travel was slow and busy for the teamsters, but there was no sign of aggressive Indians.

They started to lose daylight and moved the wagons off the road, into a small depression, and near a spring. "Get supper over before dark and snuff out the fires, boys," Ben Rhyerson said. "We'll have cold breakfast before sunrise and get movin'. Should make San Simon in a long day's ride. I'll take first watch, Snake next and then Dog-man. Let's keep the noise down to nothin'."

Thisby and Stumpy Felton had a scrawny mule deer that Dog-man shot, cut in pieces, roasting over sagebrush coals and Rhyerson had the coffee pots boiling away in no time. "We're a target," Rhyerson muttered. "Potter, this ain't a request. Keep them children of yours quiet tonight. They start screaming and yelling, I'll gag 'em."

Dog-man watched closely when supper was ready and just like Snake said, Mercy Potter brought her plate to sit with Sam Sloan instead of with Potter and the children. He saw Jesse Potter tighten up and expected there to be trouble right then. Instead, Potter brought his and the children's plates to the wagon and ate with them.

This ain't the night for it to blow up. Apache devils gonna be searchin' for us and we got an angry husband, screamin' kids, and a man needs to get the crap beat out of him. I think Ben's got half the answer. Gag them kids.

Ben Rhyerson didn't have to shake Snake awake. He was taking a long drink of cold spring water wishing there was a fire. "Haven't seen or heard nothing, Snake. Maybe we'll get lucky and Grey Wolf will hit Crabby Pete Keaton's place instead of us."

"That ain't nice to think about, but it would be better for us. Was that you moving about in camp?"

"Yeah, it was. Thought I saw someone moving around but couldn't see anything. Well, stay sharp, Mr. Snake."

Snake walked around and through the camp area, tried to pick out who was where, and ventured outside the perimeter for a walk around the entire area, in particular where the horses were. *Somebody's in with the horses. Shouldn't be.* Snake got his revolver out and slowly advanced on the single man moving slowly through the animals. *That ain't no Indian. Gonna be just as dead as one, though. Not very big.*

Snake used a pine tree for cover and got right up behind the man. *Can't be an Indian and it ain't anyone I recognize.* He eased out from the tree and shoved the pistol into the intruder's back. "One little move and you die." The man froze and Snake took a step back. "Arms wide and turn ever so slow. Who are you?"

Snake was surprised to see a boy of about twelve or thirteen years. "What on earth? Who are you boy and what are you doing out here, alone?" He pulled the heavy knife from the boy's belt and marched him into the camp area. "Better wake up, Rhyerson. We got company. Sit down, boy."

It took just minutes for the entire camp to come awake and surround Rhyerson's bedroll. "Anybody know this young-un?"

"I know him," Cheyenne said. "Mason, what are you doing out here? Told you to stay with the sheep."

Cheyenne stared at the boy. "He's my nephew, Rhyerson. My brother and I run some sheep up high and he was supposed to stay with them while Tom and I spread the word about Grey Wolf's attack on the Shaughnessy mine."

"Papa's dead," the boy cried. "The sheep, too. Indians ain't far behind me. I heard the horses and was gonna take one and ride away. Figured you were at San Simon, Uncle Cheyenne."

"You hurt?" Cheyenne asked, taking the boy in his arms. "I'm sure Tom put up a fight, but he was supposed to ride out when I did."

"He did, but the Indians chased him back. He made me run away, Uncle Cheyenne. Told me to run like the wind for San Simon."

"If Grey Wolf is on his trail, the bunch of 'em will be here shortly. Better get everybody ready." Ben Rhyerson stood up to look around. "Most of us can use the wagons for defense and a few spread out some as a welcoming committee. Stumpy, you and me with our wagon, Thisby, you and Sloan with yours. Potter, you and your wife with yours, and maybe Shaughnessy and Fairchild with you."

"Snake, you, Dog-man, and Cheyenne offer a fine welcome to our Apache neighbors. We should be able to fight off a good-sized band of hostiles. Let's dig in, boys."

"Mason, you stick with Shaughnessy. He'll take good care of you." Cheyenne said.

"I can fight," the boy said.

"I know you can, boy, but you ain't got a weapon. Now git." Cheyenne moved to join Snake and Dogman and the boy sulked off to find the miner. "Aw, hell, boy. Here, take this Remington of mine. You've shot it before." He unbuckled the gun belt and tossed it to Mason. "Shoot straight, boy and don't get shot."

"Gotta be way after midnight," Dog-man said. "Apaches don't fight at night. They'll wait for dawn and hit us hard. You're the best at finding trouble, Snake. See if you can find where they are. I'd bet that kid came down that long cut, from those mountains back up there."

"If he come from our place, he did. It's almost a natural trail down off the mountain, leading right to the springs here. Grey Wolf's probably already nested in them rocks. He'd be shooting down on us come sunrise."

"No, the wagons are off to the side and in the trees." Snake could see the layout in his mind even if he couldn't actually see it. "There's a nice ledge way up to our left that should look down on those rocks. Be a nice place for three rifles to hang out."

6

The eastern sky was getting lighter by the minute and every man checked his weapons one more time. Wouldn't be long they could see enough to shoot somebody. Dog-man and Cheyenne were huddled on the rocky shelf looking down on the wagons and camp to their right and into the defile where they expected Grey Wolf's attacking warriors to be, on their left.

"I shouldn't have let Snake go off on his own," Dog-man said. "Ain't nobody better than him at getting in trouble. If he ain't back in just a few minutes, I'm gonna go get him and whup on him bad."

Cheyenne had to chuckle. "You two been partners for some time, eh? Me and my brother are like that. Were like that," he corrected. "Gonna miss that big fella." Both men tensed up catching a glimpse of what looked like a man running through the trees below them. "That Snake?"

"Hope so," Dog-man said.

The figure found the path leading to the upper ledge and climbed up quickly. "Woke 'em up," Snake said. He was breathing hard. "Didn't mean to," he snickered. "Stepped on the one who was on watch. He won't never sleep on watch again, but they's about fifteen or so that wants my hair."

They could hear the swarming Indians racing and screaming down the narrow trail from the upper mountain, in hot pursuit. "Let's pick 'em off, one at a time, boys," Snake said. His rifle spat flame and smoke and took a warrior to the ground. The men who were huddled under the wagons let go a volley and more Apaches fell to the ground. Dog-man pumped lead from that Henry of his and Cheyenne was deadly with his rifle, too.

Arrows flew thick through the cold morning air, mixed with the howls of the wounded and screams of attacking Apache warriors. They had few guns, but their war clubs and arrows did considerable damage. The fight was quick, less than five minutes, but fierce and deadly.

"I don't think they were expecting that," Dog-man said. "They was chasing you and found all of us." Rifle and pistol fire echoed through the canyon and across the valley for just a minute or two and what was left of the marauding Grey Wolf band fled back into the mountains.

"Let's get harnessed and on the move," Ben Rhyerson yelled out. "Cold water for breakfast. Let's move it."

Everything came to a sudden stop when Mercy Potter started screaming. "No!" She screamed it, over and over. "No!"

Snake was the first one to reach her and found Sam Sloan flat on his back, a large bullet hole in the middle of his forehead. "Damn," he muttered.

He knew immediately that it had to be Potter who shot the man. So few of the attacking Apaches had firearms. Not one shot had been fired at those in the wagon train. Everything was arrows, lances, and war clubs. "Damn," he muttered again.

Snake shoved the screaming woman aside and bent down, knowing full well the man was dead. "Get her out of here before I shoot her," Snake said. Ben Rhyerson knelt down next to him. "Ain't good, Snake. Sloan brought it on himself but it's Potter and those screaming children who will face the trouble."

Snake stood up and walked out and away from the wagons, noticed Dog-Man starting to follow and waved him off. *Not this time, Dog. Gotta do this myself. Should have done what I wanted to do in the first place and beat the living tar out of that man.* He found a dead Apache, reached down inside his boot and pulled a revolver out. *Gonna miss you, partner. Saved me more than once.* He opened the cylinder and replaced one of the bullets with a spent casing and put the gun in the hand of the dead Indian.

When he got back to where they were starting to hitch up the teams, he called Rhyerson over. "Anything being said?"

"Talk's already gotten around to hanging Potter for open murder."

"Let's you and me make sure none of those murdering 'Paches is still alive before we shove off." He and Ben Rhyerson walked off through the rocks and brush, checking each body they came to. It was, of course, Ben Rhyerson who discovered the only Apache within ten miles or so who had a weapon.

"Look here, Snake. He's got a sidearm." Rhyerson hollered back at those finishing the harnessing to cone see. "Look," he said several times. Cheyenne knelt down and picked up the weapon, opening the cylinder and seeing one shot had been fired. He looked up at Snake, over at Rhyerson and put the gun down.

"One shot fired," Cheyenne said. "Maybe it wasn't Potter what shot Sloan. I'd sure rather believe that," he almost whispered.

"We'll talk about this when we get to San Simon. Right now, we got to get these wagons on the road. Them Indians are gonna re-group and come down on us again. Anyone can't keep up gets left behind." That last comment was aimed straight at Mercy Potter and she shrank back from his intense look.

Shaughnessy and Fairchild rode with Mrs. Potter and the two boys rode with their father. Not a word had been exchanged between the Potters since the discovery of Sloan's body, but not a minute was spent not hearing Mercy Potter crying. "At least the kids have a father," Snake muttered. He stepped into the stirrup, heaved himself into the saddle and faced the day with a smile.

***

"Ain't gonna take the time to cook tonight. Just gonna eat two pounds of raw meat and go to sleep," Snake said, shaking out his bedroll. The wagons rolled into San Simon late in the day, everyone tired from moving the animals much faster than they wanted to go and moved just as quickly to get animals settled and camp made up.

"Need to work out the Potter question before we eat, folks," Rhyerson said. "I know how tired we are, but a man is dead and another man has been accused of killing him. Finding that Indian with a gun, with one round fired, changes what we first believed. Keep that fire going, Mason, and we'll talk." The boy got right to it, glad to be included in the conversation.

"Don't think there's too much to talk about, Ben." Snake poured some whiskey into his coffee and slouched down against a broken tree limb. "Sloan was shot from the front during an Indian attack. Don't think Potter or anyone else would turn his back on an Indian attack in order to shoot the man."

There was a lot of long Texas pauses in his speech, which was followed by heads nodding and no talking back. "Everyone in favor of what Snake just said, say aye." Rhyerson didn't have to ask for a no vote. "That's settled then. Potter, how you and the missus settle things is up to you. I think it's best though that you find your own way to Tucson. It's just a few days from here."

"Let's go spread our blankets by the creek, Dog. I'm just about fed up with people. Away from the station, away from everything." The San Simon Station was host to stage lines, freight companies and immigrants making their way to southern California. There were saloons, a trade goods outlet and more than one business offering meats, vegetables and dry goods.

"Don't want to know how you pulled this off, Snake, but I do want you to know I'm damn proud to be your partner. You got a real way about you, sometimes."

"Man at the trade station sold me some fresh young beef they just slaughtered," Snake said. He ignored Dog-man's comments. "We'll warm a couple of these steaks and fill our cups with whiskey and talk about Tucson. We'll be there in a couple of days."

"Gonna buy me a new shirt, maybe blue. Talk to a couple of the business people, you know, at the feed stores or blacksmiths, find out about the area. I like these mountains we're in right now, cept'n' for the folks who live here. They are not neighborly, Snake."

"Nope, they ain't. Cheyenne and Mason already lit out. Seen 'em ride off right after the Potter meeting. Sure would like to follow, but we got an obligation to old George Dawson."

"Yup." Dog-man raked some coals back from their little fire and laid a frying pan on them. "We've had beans and side-meat so often I don't think I can remember what these steaks are gonna taste like."

"Just take the moo out of mine, Dog, and it'll be fine." Snake took a long drink of cool creek water and filled the tin cup with whiskey. "That creek there, must run year-round. Put a sprinkle of water to this country and you could grow some good beef. Sloan wasn't wrong about breeding horses and mules, either. Steep and rocky, every blessed bush's got a gazillion thorns, and the bugs sting and bite, but if you put some water down, you could grow cows."

"We know how to do that, too," Dog-man said. "You thinkin' of settling down? I'd still like to see what all the fuss about California is. But runnin' a nice herd of horned critters has always been in the back of my head."

"You thinking about cows or are you remembering that selfish little girl back in Colorado?" Snake said. He had a straight look on his face but had to chuckle. "Me? I'm just thinkin' about lookin'," Snake said. "Let's eat. Them steaks got a good smell to 'em."

"Rhyerson wants to pull out at sunrise. We still got some rough country to go through but hopefully not so many angry neighbors to put up with."

"Best part of the trip comin' up, Dog. No screaming children for two days at least. I want to find a cantina with chilies and cold beer."

"I'll take the cold beer. We got a set of high mountains we gotta cross yet. Talked with Stumpy and he said the road is in good condition all the way in. Cold beer, eh? I vote yay."

7

The two days from San Simon to Tucson were un-eventful with the exception of the San Pedro River crossing. Sucking mud almost ruined one of the teams, but nobody was hurt and none of the freight was damaged. Potter and the two boys stayed with the train, but Mercy Potter elected to stay in San Simon. It was the best decision, most agreed. The children were rather well-behaved, even.

"This is an old town, Snake." They were in the heart of Tucson, looking at buildings as old as two hundred years. "Spanish built all this according to Rhyerson. Glad we made this trip even if it wasn't all nice and easy."

"Long valley, high mountains close by, and fair water, Dog. Ben Rhyerson paid us off," Snake said. He handed Dog-man an envelope. "Dawson's a man of his word. There's a note in there saying we got a job any time we want one. What I want is a platter of Mexican food this high and filled with green chilis."

"There's a feed and hardware store, Snake, and a cantina right across the plaza." Dog-man was pointing across the busy plaza. Tucson was an ancient town, settled by Spanish, but originally by those that came before the Apache and other local Indians.

"Let's go." Dog-man nudged his horse, and they rode into a brightly colored plaza, anchored by a magnificent church at one end, and surrounded all around by commercial interests. Mexican music flowed like sweet syrup from the cantina along with the aromatic pleasures to be found inside.

"Haven't had some good chilies since we left Las Cruces," Snake said. They tied their horses off, brushed off as much dust as they could and sauntered in. Three musicians were strolling through, one with a guitar, one with a potato bug guitar, and one with a trumpet, playing wonderful music.

"Now is the hard part, Dog. Do we eat first, or find a charming señorita and dance away the rest of the day?" He did a quick little two-step, bowed to one of the serving girls and laughed out loud. "I vote for eating first."

"Shaughnessy and Fairchild are right over there. Let's join 'em," Dog-man said. "They probably need some friendly talk after losing everything to the Apaches."

Snake and Dog-man settled in with the two miners, ordered enough food for four, flagons of beer and looked around at the crowd. "A little bit of everything in here," Dog-man said. "Those boys there are surely cow men and those over there. Teamsters, miners, businessmen, and pretty girls serving good food."

"Sounds like you've found a home," Sean Shaughnessy said. "Me and Fairchild spend some good times in here. Americans, Mexicans and Frenchmen mostly. The freight road into California is busy year around and they're talking of building a railroad real soon."

"Where does that freight road go?" Dog-man asked.

"Heads over to Gila Bend, across the biggest river you ever seen, down at Yuma and on into California. Boats on the river come up from Mexico with freight coming this way. They're freighted north into Phoenix and Prescott, too," Shaughnessy said.

"I'd like to see that," Dog-man said. "Boats coming through the desert from Mexico." He had a quizzical look, but nobody said anything and he let it go.

"What are yours and Fairchild's plans now that you've been burnt out? Plan on going back?" Snake asked.

"Gotta go back. Gold and silver in those rocks. We spent most of the morning buying what we think we'll need to reopen. Getting it there will be hardest. We'll need a freighter with six-up and a good mule skinner to get us back, but we're going. What about you boys?"

"We ain't making no decisions about nothing for at least three days," Snake said. "Gonna get the grit out of our teeth, gotta get Dog-man a new shirt and look this country over some. Been to that feed and supply store over there?"

"Puny Russell's been here as long as the Spanish, I think," Aaron Fairchild laughed. "Knows this country inside and out. Square dealer, too. His wife's family dates from the original Spanish Conquistadores. Rosie has a fiery temper, was a real looker forty years ago and rules Puny something terrible. He loves it, though."

"Enough palavering, enough fire in my belly, it's time to meet Puny Russell," Snake said.

The four men shook hands and Snake and Dog-man walked their horses across the plaza. The Tucson Mercantile took up a great section of street front, equipment and material spread across the boardwalk and into the street. "Old Sean said that this Puny feller knows just about everything that's going on in the valley," Dog-man said. "He sure has a lot of merchandise for sale."

The aisles inside were narrow, goods stacked high on both sides and a long sales counter with even more merchandise spread about, in the rear of the store. Picks, axes, carbide and dynamite in one section, along with plows, harness, shovels and hoes in another. "Even got pots and pans, needle and thread," Dog-man laughed.

"Evening, boys. Didn't I see you come in with the Dawson freighters earlier? What can I help you with?"

Puny Russell wasn't puny. The man towered over Snake and Dog-man, probably weighed in at two fifty or more and had a chest and shoulders like a prairie buffalo. He hadn't had a haircut or beard trim in years and his dark red hair, sprinkled with shards of silver, was braided and hung almost to his waist, while his beard flowed and ebbed with every facial expression, which was mostly friendly and open.

"Yes, came in with Dawson but not going back," Dog-man said. "Want to know more about this country and been told you're the man to talk to."

"You look more like cow men than freighters," Puny said. "Got some fine ranches in the valley.

Good water, good grass. The RT, a little north of here's looking for a couple of men. Rufus Theron's a cusser. Wife's name is April. You want to meet the man, he's out back looking at some fencing I got in." Puny was far more friendly than most people Snake had met in towns and nodded to the man.

"Got a nice spread, does he?"

"Could have." Russell said, and shook his head, almost sadly. "Couple of sections and runs some fine Mexican cross beef. He don't tolerate much nonsense and has a hard time keeping a crew. Don't mean to steer you off but thought you should know that."

Rufus Theron was looking at spools of barbed wire and nodding. "Might want some of this to keep the goats out of April's garden. About all it's good for. Ain't much for fences. Who you got with you?"

"I'm Snake, this is my partner, Dog-man. Heard you might be looking for a couple of hands."

"Got business in town tomorrow. Come to the ranch the day after and we'll talk some about that. Puny, draw 'em a map on how to find the place. Got to get to the land office before it closes. Snake, eh? Is it Mr. Snake."

"Just Snake will do fine, Mr. Theron. We'll see you in two days."

***

"Hotel or camp?" Dog-man asked as they stepped out of the store and into early evening. Dog-man was wearing a brand new, royal blue with white piping, shirt.

"Follow that stream north and camp. Glad we stopped, though. Got yourself a new blue shirt and we got coffee, beans and sidemeat. I got a whole bag of dried chilies, Dog. We'll find some trees not too far from the creek and settle in for a couple of days. What did you think of old Rufus T. Theron?"

The valley spread out north as they rode. High mountains to their right and a lot of desert to their north and west. "We've met worse, Snake. From the looks of him, he gets right in and works with his crew. I like that in a man."

"He ain't a swaggerin' man, either. He'll let his place speak for itself and let us prove ourselves, too. Map makes it look about fifteen miles out. See them big trees way off the road? Let's make that our new home."

Fresh water, plenty of shade, grass for the horses and the men were settled in quickly. "Think Puny Russell was trying to shy us off the Theron place? Quite a warning, seemed to me." Dog-man was leaning back on the trunk of a tree, his tin-cup full of hot coffee with a generous splash of whiskey in it.

"Wondering." Snake said. "Thinking of Jesse Potter, too. Two screaming kids, no wife, trying to start a new life. Sloan got what he deserved, but Potter's gotta pay a big price. Puny said Theron's got a wife. Hope she's a good one. Let's ride out toward the Theron place tomorrow. See what it looks like. We can come back along the base of those mountains."

"Ain't heard this many words from you in some time, Snake. You're about as glad to be rid of those wagons as I am." Dog-man caught the quick smile from his partner and poured some more whiskey in his tin cup. "Gonna like these next few days."

The sun was making its final plunge into the far west desert. The mountains to their east were in blazing color, spires of rock, standing thousands of feet and gleaming in these final rays. Long dark shadows indicated canyons, passes and ridges and along the base of the mountains, a smudge of smoke here and there, from a ranch or farm. "Hope some of that smoke ain't Apache smoke," Dog-man said.

"Hard not to like country like this." Snake filled his cup, added some whiskey and lounged back against a big rock. "Got bit by at least fourteen bushes and twenty five bugs riding out here and I swear at least one of them tall cactus trees lunged at me once. Apache's are right, you know, trying to keep it all for themselves."

"Tomorrow's gonna come fast, Snake," Dog-man said. "Sun's about gone and I ain't been this tired in a long time. Night-night." Snake had to chuckle, hearing soft snoring within moments.

***

"Ain't a bad looking home place, Snake. Big house spread out like that, barns and corrals in good condition." They were on a small hill about a mile from the RT home ranch, lookin down on the operation. "Must be the bunkhouse off to the left there and the garden Theron said he needed the fence for in the back of the house."

"Wonder where the cattle are? Ain't seen none riding in, can't see none looking around. Puny said the man had two sections, should see some, anyway."

"Let's ride toward those mountains. Maybe we'll see some." Dog-man noticed that the corrals near the barns were empty, too. "If he's got a crew, they don't have many horses to draw from. I think we'll need to be a little bit careful when we're talking to old man Theron."

"That's a high ridge we're looking at, Dog. Let's ride along its base north for a while. See what we can see." They rode across the rolling flats of the valley, crossing several deep arroyos, some with water still flowing and up to the intimidating face of rock. Turning north they could see the ridge bend itself into rolling foothills leading into high mountains.

"Moved through many miles of open country, Dog and ain't seen a single head of beef, except for those few near the water. Might want to remember what Puny said about Mr. Theron."

Dog-man just nodded in agreement, enjoying the beauty of the desert. "I'd think this was Indian country, Snake, but haven't seen any sign. Nobody was talking trouble yesterday. Let's get back out on the valley floor and keep our eyes open."

"Got the same feelings. If Theron can't keep a crew and his cattle scatter on him and if the Apaches know that, he won't have a herd for long. Wouldn't be no need to send war parties out if all they have to do is gather the cattle."

***

"Well, Rufus, come in. I've been expecting you. Your note said you're in a bind of some kind?" Major William Fleming owned the Bank of Tucson, was originally from Virginia but had come west years before the big war that sundered the country. He picked up the rank from organizing a militia group to defend against marauding Indians and Mexican bandits. Fleming bought and charmed his way into being one of Tucson's leading citizens.

"Indians been stealing my cattle, getting more and more brave about it and I can't keep a crew because of it. Ain't gonna make my payment, Major, unless I get some help fighting off the Indians. They burned out some miners, attacked freight wagons and stole cattle."

"I know, Rufus. I know," Fleming said. He showed Theron to a chair and sat down behind his desk. He offered a cigar and took one for himself as well. "We got a beautiful valley here, a good economy, and more and more people moving in. I've sent wires to the army, but they have problems up north as well."

He motioned for one of the bank clerks to bring some coffee. "Now, let's talk about this other problem of yours. You're already behind on your payments, Rufus. I can't let it go much longer. I'm not a threatening man, as I hope you know, but I can't carry you too much longer. It isn't the Indians alone that is your problem with keeping hired hands. It's the way you treat them."

Major Fleming's reputation went two ways. Those who owed him money and were able to make their payments on time had no trouble with the man. The others considered Fleming ruthless, mean-spirited, and ready to pounce at a moment's notice. The men who worked for Fleming were not among Tucson's favorites. Drunks, thieves, and a few down and out gamblers were used to encourage the payments of loans.

Theron grimaced at the Major's words, had heard them before and braced for Fleming turning him down on a loan extension. "I expect the men I hire to give me full measure. I pay them and feed them."

The major pulled an ornate flask from his desk when the coffee arrived. "This is brandy from the grapes of France, Rufus. Let's have a drink and talk about how we can get you out of this mess. You're a good man with cattle, a good family man, too. You just don't have much niceness in you when it comes to people who work for you." Fleming smiled and sipped his coffee. "Strong words, I know, but the truth, you have to admit."

"I guess you might be somewhat right but what do you do when a man won't do the job the way I want it done? Gotta be strong with your help or they won't do the job."

"Sometimes, my friend, there's more than one way to get a job done. You can hover over a horse, yell at him, threaten him, and even strike him. Maybe get the horse to do what you want. Or you can take the time to show the horse what you want and allow the horse to learn what to do. A man isn't a whole lot different, Rufus. Most people want to do a good job." He looked across the desk at the sad man and wondered what kind of growing up he had to endure.

The way he treats his hands may be a reflection off the way he was treated as a youngster. The banker was raised in an interesting family on a well-established Texas ranch. His mother was cold, demanding, and quick with a switch. Major Fleming's father, too, owned a bank. More than one, actually. He learned his economics from his father. If a man pays what he owes, treat him kindly. Otherwise, make him pay, one way or another.

"Let your hands know what you want without

demanding things they don't know, teach them the right way, feed them well, give them good horses to ride, and maybe they'll stay with you."

"Ain't my way, Major, but I guess you could be right. Will you give me one more extension? If I can get my steers to the Gila Bend market this fall, I'll be able to get caught up and then some. Just one more extension. There are two fine looking cow men coming to the ranch tomorrow and I'll be fair with them."

Fleming snickered, knowing he'd run 'em off in days, would never get the herd to the sale, and Fleming would own the ranch before winter. The major stood up and offered his hand. "I know you'll try, Rufus and I hope you know this will be the last extension. If they are good hands, let them be good hands. Maybe they don't do things the same way you do, but still get the job done. That's the point, isn't it? To get the job done.

"Come. I'll see you out and I hope our next visit will be more to both of our likings." Fleming's likings were to have that ranch back on the market and Theron off the property.

It was a long ride out to the RT spread and Rufus Theron spent most of it wondering if Major Fleming really knew what he was talking about. Theron's father beat him with harness leather if he didn't do exactly what he was supposed to do, and remembered his father telling him stories about being whipped when he was a child.

"You'll learn to do it right or be bruised and bloody for the rest of your life is what the old man would say," Theron said, right out loud. "He whupped on ma and all us kids, whupped on the mules, too, but

we learned to do it right, whatever the job was." He
went through periods of deep contemplation and
moments of fury, wondering why Major Fleming
thought he should be easier on his hands.

"He led men into battle against Mexicans and
Indians, so he must have some knowledge about
making men do what needed to be done." It was
a long ride home. The concept of making men do
what needed to be done instead of teaching them do
what needed to be done hadn't sunk in.

8

"We got the extension, April. Thank God, we got the extension." Rufus Theron was sitting at the large kitchen table late that evening. He rode well into the evening after his meeting with the major and the let down was starting. The pressure, fully understanding that he could lose the ranch, the herd, everything had been heavy for months. The children had eaten and been sent off, and there were no hands to feed. It was he and April at the table. "I could feel the load lift from my heart when Fleming said yes."

"I'm so glad, Rufe. You work so hard and you've said we've got a good herd to sell this year. I have chicken and dumplings hot for you. Fresh corn, too. Wash up and it'll be ready."

"I don't like dumplings, April. You know I don't like 'em. Why do you fix things I don't like, woman? Put the chicken on a plate with some corn." He stormed across the room to wash up, sloshing water all about.

"The children love chicken and dumplings, Rufe. I didn't know you were coming home tonight. We were thinking you'd come home in the morning." She tried not to but whined. She forced herself not to cry this time. "I don't know why you get so angry over little things like this."

Rufus Theron didn't say another word, just wolfed down his supper, got up and went to bed, an angry man. It was then that April Theron allowed herself to cry, alone, at an empty kitchen table. It hadn't always been this way, she remembered. It wasn't until Geneva was born, twelve years ago, that Rufe got so one way about things. "Why?" She cried, softly.

They had talked about children and, as she remembered it, he never said no to the idea. It was during the pregnancy that he became angry about the whole program. They moved to Arizona Territory after Geneva's birth and settled on this property. "Not one thing in life has suited him since her birth," she muttered. "Including me. It's time for changes to be made."

There were two more children and he was mean to all of them, to her and to anyone foolish enough to go to work for him. She sat, sobbing quietly, wondering why she let his behavior continue and she didn't leave. "Why?" She almost choked it out. She justified not leaving because of the children and at the same time she knew they didn't really have a father, either, not with the way Rufus was.

I have to get out before he ruins the children. He's so angry, all the time, willing to hurt anyone who even slightly crosses him. He's ruined me, but I can't let him ruin the children. The stove was cold when April finally walked into their spacious bedroom. *He was almost loving when we were first together.*

***

"Mommy, Daddy, wake up. Wake up." Geneva, twelve-years-old, was standing at the foot of the bed screaming. "Indians!" She screamed the word out and Rufus was out of bed and in his pants and boots, running for the kitchen and his shotgun. He could hear horses running, could hear the howls of Indians racing around the large ranch house, grabbed the double-barreled shotgun and raced to a window.

There were no less than ten that he could see, wildly painted, brandishing war clubs and flaming torches. Most carried bows and had quivers full of arrows. April ran in and Rufus screamed at her to get a rifle, screamed at Geneva to get ammunition for both off them. Hank, ten-years-old, raced in, eyes like saucers, staring out the window. "Indians. Look, Ma. Indians."

April grabbed him back and told him to go to his room and stay there, raced into the living room and brought two rifles back into the kitchen. Geneva had boxes of ammunition on the kitchen table. Rufus loaded his shotgun, pocketed half a dozen shells and moved to one of the kitchen windows, left of the doorway.

April had a rifle loaded and moved to the other window. "Load the other rifle and be ready to hand it to me," she said. "We've practiced this, Geneva, but it's for real this time."

"I know, Mama, I'm ready," she said. She gasped when the window in front of her mother shattered. April whirled and shot an intruder, point blank. He had a torch and dropped it onto the wide wooden kitchen porch as he fell. The wooden porch was tinder dry and April knew the walls of the house would soon be in flames.

Only a few of the Indians had firearms, the rest carried bows and arrows, war clubs and lances. Arrows were thudding into the walls and coming through the windows, but luckily not hitting anyone in the kitchen. April was a crack shot with her Winchester and knocked two warriors from their horses but was soon driven from the window by the flames. The porch and wall at the window were burning furiously.

Rufus's shotgun belched fire and smoke constantly when all at once the Indians made a dash out of the area. Heavy gunfire followed them out as two riders descended on the farmyard, firing and yelling at the top of their lungs. "Run, you red devils, run." Dog-man was screaming as loud as the marauders.

Snake saw the fire and jumped from his horse, grabbed what was left of the torch and threw it away from the building. He ran hard to the well and filled a bucket when Rufus ran onto the porch. "Hurry, man, hurry."

Rufus ran to the well and filled another bucket when Snake returned with the empty. They continued for several minutes, getting the fire knocked down and out. April and Geneva came out onto the porch and Dog-man rode back into the farmyard. "Anyone hurt?" He asked. "Not sure how far those boys will run. Might want to get back inside if they decide to come back."

"They'll be back," Snake said. "You can count on that." He looked at Geneva, standing next to her mother. "Hello, little one. That's a mighty big rifle you're carryin'. You a good shooter, are you?" He had a wide smile and his eyes were dancing at the sight.

"I'm the loader," she said. "Mama's the shooter. I load and she shoots. Just like we practice."

"Well, I'd say you're a fine team, then." Snake started to say more when they heard screaming from Indians riding down on them from the north. "Inside," Snake yelled. A steel tipped arrow sank into the door just as it slammed closed. Dog-man and Snake took one window, April and Geneva the other, and Rufus eased the door open to let the shotgun have its say.

"Ain't but five of 'em," Dog-man said. His Henry barked and he chuckled. "I mean, four." Geneva giggled and Dog-man grabbed her and did a little dance of celebration. Rufus flew into a rage.

"This isn't a game, Geneva. You'll feel my belt when this is over. You concentrate on getting that rifle loaded." He tuned to Dog-man. "Don't you be talking with my daughter like that, mister."

"You're welcome," Dog-man said. "Glad we could help. Ready, Snake? Seems we've worn out our welcome here." He stepped back from the window, reloaded the Henry, checked the load in his revolver and walked to the door. "We'll kill the rest on the way out if you like." Any semblance of friendliness was wiped off his face. Snake was sure he was about to shoot the man.

"No!" April yelled it out. "Rufus, that's no way to talk to these men who have helped us so much. No," she said again. She grabbed little Geneva up and held her tight and turned to Dog-man.

"Please, you've done us such a wonderful favor. Rufus, you cannot continue this way. You've got

Geneva crying, you've got Indians trying to kill us and burn us out and you're chasing away the men who have come to help. These men have saved our lives, Rufe." April gathered herself up, squared her shoulders and glared at her husband. She had never stood up to the man, never questioned his actions, and Rufus Theron was in a rage. No woman had ever talked to him that way.

"This angry way of yours must stop," she commanded. "Come, Geneva, let's make sure the rifles are loaded." She was standing at her window, rifle at the ready and watched the last of the Indian raiders ride out of the farmyard. "They're gone," she whispered. She looked first at Dog-man, then to Snake, shook her head slowly and tried to smile.

"We've been having hard times," she said. Snake gave her a big smile, pulled a chair out and indicated she should sit. "Trouble keeping hands, trouble from losing animals to the Indians, and a small herd that needs to be moved to the sale at Gila Bend. Rufus didn't mean what he said. We're far more than just grateful for your coming when you did." She turned in her chair to say something to her husband.

Rufus Theron turned away from her, anger spreading through his body like a virus. He opened the kitchen door and stepped onto the porch, his shotgun hanging by one hand. He wasn't going to be a part of this, wasn't going to listen to her talk to hired hands like that. He took one step and caught an arrow, high in his right leg. He tumbled to the ground, howling in pain. Snake rushed through the door and killed the already wounded warrior who was notching a second arrow. "Get him back inside, Dog-man. I'll check on the rest of these, make sure they ain't playing dead. Be gentle with him," Snake said. The slight grin gave Dog-man the chuckles.

Dog-man and April helped get Rufus back up-right and into the house. April led them into the bedroom and got him laid out, that arrow sticking straight up. "Better get me something to stop the bleeding and something to stop the infection that's sure to follow," Dog-man said. "You just settle in, Rufus, coz this is gonna hurt."

April ran for the kitchen to get a pan of hot water, told Geneva to get sheets and medicine and came back in, in time to see Dog-man rip the pants leg open. The arrow point of sharp steel, had buried itself in Rufus's leg bone. Dog-man used his knife to cut the shaft off a couple of inches from the skin so he could be moved.

"Indians like to dip their arrows in poisons and putrid stuff. Even if the shot itself doesn't kill, the infection or poison will. We need to get this man to a doctor."

April was cleaning the wound, putting a salve on it and wrapped it as best she could. Geneva stood at her side, handing her whatever she asked for. "You two are quite a team," he said. "Hope you're around if I get hurt. We got to get this man to town, Miz Theron. That arrow's stuck in the bone."

"You called my mom Miz Theron. It's Mrs.," Geneva said. "Mama wants us to learn to speak proper."

Dog-man smiled and sat down on the edge of the bed. "All right, how's this. Need a doc for this, Mrs. Theron. Can't just push the arrow on through. Got a buggy or wagon we can hitch up?" Geneva giggled and Dog-man pretended to look hurt. The bedroom was large and featured a window on one wall and racks and shelves for hanging clothing and folded clothes, too. The bed was rough-hewn logs, tied and nailed, holding a sack mattress. "A wagon would be best."

"Yes," April said. "I'll tend to him." She wondered how on earth her little girl, could have such trust in these two men, when she often had a hard time showing any love for her own father. *Geneva knows instinctively that these are good men. I wish I'd had some inner knowledge about Rufus before we married. This one's really good looking but it's that tall skinny one that's got something. What?* She caught herself and finished wrapping the wound.

"Geneva, take these men to the barn and help them get the spring wagon ready." She offered a smile when she turned to Dog-man. "She'll show you everything." April's eyes were streaming with tears as she said this despite the smile on her face. She'd never seen anything like the way this man simply took control of a situation. No screaming. No threats. No slaps or back-hands.

Geneva took Dog-man's hand and led him out to the barn. "The wagon's in the back with all the harness and the team is in the corral." She was tall for her twelve years, skinny as a rail, with flowing blondish hair like her mother's. A cascade of freckles worked their way across a pretty face, which lit up when she smiled. Big green eyes sparkled in the sunlight. "Mama has been teaching me how to drive the team. They love to run."

"You and your mama are close, aren't you," Dog-man said. He was still angry at the way Rufus had snarled at his daughter, threatened her with a beating and chastised him. "We'll need to let that team of yours run if we're gonna get your pa to the doctor in time. I'll get the horses."

Just a few days ago, when we finally got loose from the Potter family and those screaming children, I didn't ever want to be around a kid ever again. And just look at me, lovin' this kid. The screaming kids had a loving father and this kid has a bastard for a father. Life is interesting. Me and Snake are gonna have to talk about this.

Snake brought Rufus out, April right behind with blankets. She had seven-year old Terry hanging on one side, and ten-year-old Hank on the other. It took everyone to get the injured man up and into the bed of the spring wagon. Every movement or jolt to that arrow shaft brought howls of pain from the man. The blankets were laid out and April helped get him comfortable. Dog-man tied his horse to the back of the wagon and took up the reins.

The two younger children also helped their mother get Rufus as comfortable as possible, had gourds of water under the blankets and were willing to help, despite the man's constant crying out from the pain. "It's not going to be a nice ride to town, children," April said.

"It's all right, Mama," Hank said. "I was scared when I saw all those Indians. We'll help you keep Papa safe. Who are these men?"

"They saved us, Hank. Better get moving," April said.

"I'll drive," Geneva said. "You and that tall man need to be on your horses in case the Indians come back."

"These are strong horses, Geneva. You sure you can handle them?" Dog-man looked back over his shoulder and caught a grin from April.

"Gonna be a mule-skinner when she grows up," she said. "She's got a way with animals that neither her father nor I have. They seem to listen to her."

"Animals know when your heart is good," Snake said. "Keep him from bleeding hard and if you need help, one of us will jump in with you." Snake looked over at Geneva. "All right, little one, take us to town."

It was a fast fifteen miles. Rufus spent most of the ride unconscious and Geneva became Dog-man's best friend. He rode alongside the wagon the entire trip, ready to jump in if trouble came their way. It didn't and even as quick as they were moving, the two talked a lot. "You can drive any wagon of mine anytime you want, little lady." He jumped off his horse and took the lead rope and tied the team off in front of the doctor's office while Snake helped get Rufus out of the wagon and inside.

"We haven't been properly introduced, ma'am," Dog-man said. They were standing in the room where Rufus was taken, watching Doctor Phinieus McCarthy work to get the arrow out. "All the shooting and problems kinda set our manners aside. I'm Dog-man and this other grubby feller is Snake. We was coming out to talk with your husband about hiring on. Guess that's out of the question, seein' as how he don't much care for us none."

"I'm Mrs. Theron and right now, it's very much in the question. What you two did was wonderful and since Rufe isn't going to be doing much work around the place for some time, I'd be more than happy if you would consider coming on board. According to Rufe, we've got a small herd of fine steers we want to take to the big market in Gila

Bend soon and no hired hands."

Dog-man looked over at Snake who was having a hard time holding Rufus down while Doc McCarthy extracted the remains of the arrow. "I'd rather not be talked to that way, again," Snake said. "Me and Dog-man have pushed a lot of beef through rough country, Mrs. Theron, and this wasn't our first meeting with angry Indians, neither. Working for you and that charming little muleskinner daughter of yours would be a pleasure."

"Then we'd best get back to the ranch before the Indians discover we're not there and burn us out." She looked at McCarthy who shook his head.

"He can't go back, April. Infection's already set in. Probably dipped that arrow into something nasty. They like to do that so even a slight wound will infect and kill. He's gotta stay here. I understand, though that you have to get back. He'll be fine here." Dr. McCarthy was cleaning the wound with some powerful medicine that had Rufus almost screaming for mercy. "Hush, now, Rufus. When it hurts like that, it means it's working." He had a wicked smile on his face and Dog-man looked at Snake to see the same kind of smile.

"Gotta remember that, Doc. If it hurts, it means it's working." He couldn't hold the laughter as they walked from the room.

9

"Ain't been nobody in the bunkhouse for a spell, I'm afraid," April said, getting the door open. Dust, cobwebs, and almost filth filled the place. "Rufus would never let any of us clean up in here. Always said if the hired hands wanted to live in filth, it was their choice. We'll leave this for the time being."

"It's a mess and you're right, we'll get to this later. Got dead one's out here in the heat," Snake said.

"Come to the kitchen when you're through. Supper and talk time," April said. She and the children walked back to the house. It was Geneva who turned to look at Snake and Dog-man. Dog-man saw the smile as a welcome, Snake saw it coming from a courageous little girl needing a father.

"These people are in more trouble than even we could get into," Snake said. He waved to Geneva and picked up a shovel. "If we weren't us, Dog-man, I'd suggest we just ride on out."

"Might regret this, Snake, but we are us."

"Don't want to, but I keep comparing Mrs. Theron to Mrs. Potter. I want to know one of them and hope I never see the other." Snake said.

It took several hours to bury the dead Indians and clean up the mess from the intense fight before Snake and Dog-man would be able to get the bunkhouse halfway livable. "Longest day I've put in in some time," Snake said as he washed at the well and walked into the kitchen at the big house. Terry, eight and Hank, ten, were wrestling and laughing and Dog-man pretended to join in. Geneva looked at Snake and shook her head, but finally had to giggle.

Snake took a chair as did April. "You've lost steers to the Indians?" Snake asked. Dog-man broke free of the little one's and joined them at the table.

"Supper coming soon, men. Yes, Rufus thinks so. The herd is really dispersed since we haven't had any hands to work them."

"What you're saying is, you don't really know what you have." Dog-man shook his head, watching April's head hang down. "Do you ride? Know your way around a cow? Throw a rope?"

"Can't rope very well. Rufus says it ain't for women to do. I can help move cattle, though. Me and Geneva probably don't do it right, but we can get cows from one corral to another."

"First thing in the morning, we'll locate as many of your animals as we can and get them moving back here. Do you have an estimate on how many animals you think you have? Sure would help. Where is this market you were going to bring them to? How far is it and when do we need to be there? This is hot country and a beef can lose a lot of weight if he's moved too fast."

April walked over to the table with a Dutch oven full of beef stew and set it down. "I think we have about a hundred heifers, Dog-man." She couldn't smile and just shook her head. "I know we have some bulls that Rufus says are highly prized. He's not very open about things and gets angry if I ask too many questions." Tears were running down her cheeks as she sat down. Geneva wrapped her skinny little arms around her mama and held her tight.

"A hundred heifers? You don't know how many steers? That's what get sold." Snake's frustration was showing. "I'm not being mean or taking cheap shots, but that husband of yours has let you down, Mrs. Theron." *She don't stand a chance, now I've made her cry and somebody needs to whack old Theron across the side of his head. Shoot the bastard.*

"Papa says it will take two weeks to move the herd to Gila Bend and the sale is coming up in four or five weeks." Geneva walked over to the wall and pointed at a calendar hanging with dates circled. "He said it would take five good men to make the drive."

"We'll know that when we know how many critters will be in the drive," Dog-man said. "We'll start finding that answer first thing in the morning."

The two men left and April sat at the table, crying softly. "He's right, you know," she held Geneva, rocked back and forth. "Rufe has never talked about the steers, only the heifers. I wonder why? It's time for us to get tough, Geneva. Tough and mean if we're going to save this ranch."

***

"Ain't this pickle barrel full," Snake said, flopping down on a cot in the bunkhouse. "We got two good men, a somewhat weak woman, a kid muleskinner and two more kids to boot, to move a hundred or more steers across open desert for two weeks. And we don't know where them steers are. Or even if there are any. You got us in a mess this time, Dog-man."

"Nope, not me this time." Dog-man stretched out on his cot and lit a cheroot. "Woman's a good cook. Good woman, good kids, jerk for a husband. Just the opposite of the Potter family."

"That skinny little girl is the smartest one in the family," Snake said. "Three kids and a wife to feed and care for and Rufus P. Theron can't keep a crew. Sumpin' wrong with that man."

"Something wrong with the woman for putting up with him. I almost dropped him; you understand. No call to talk to us that way after we saved their scrawny hides. I guess we've all but signed on for this drive, though. Good thing we already got money coz I don't think we're gonna get paid for this drive," Dog-man said.

"We'll find water in the morning and most likely find a bunch of cattle. Might take three or four days to get them's that'r still around. Most were ate up by the Indians, I imagine. If Theron treats everyone looking to come to work for him as he treated us, he deserves to lose this ranch. On top of that, Dog, why does that woman stay with him? She ain't hard to look at. I've noticed you thinkin' so."

"What's a woman gonna do to keep three kids alive and well?"

"Probably more than Theron, Dog. Probably more. None of them kids is getting enough to eat and they got beef on the hoof. That man ain't right."

First light found the two men brushing out their

horses, wishing there had been a cook stove in the bunkhouse. "We change that when we get back. Coffee is a necessity, Dog. Can't make the morning without my coffee. We shoulda just lit a fire."

The loud ringing of an iron triangle interrupted the conversation. "Well, now," Dog-man said. "Sounds like the cry of a neglected pot of coffee, Snake. Better get to its rescue, eh?" They found the two boys still wrestling but April and Geneva had a full table of hot cakes, side meat, fresh biscuits and coffee ready for them.

"Been a long time since I had hands to feed, gentlemen. Feels good." April had a face full of smile as she ushered them to the table, but Dog-man also saw red rimmed eyes looking back at him. "Do you think those Indians will be back?"

"I'm afraid so," Snake said. "They don't like it much, gettin' run off like that. What kind of relationship do you have with Puny Russell? We could use at least two more men, three would be better."

"Puny has helped us considerable, but I don't have any way of paying for more help. What kind of wage did Rufus offer you boys? We've missed our land payments twice now, not made a drive to Gila Bend in two years, either. There simply isn't any money in the tin box right now."

Dog-man saw the anger in Snake's face, felt his own building. "Two years without taking the herd to market? Why do you breed beef cattle if you don't sell them?" Dog-man wanted to say a lot more, but he was talking to April, not Rufus. It was Rufus he wanted to scream obscenities at, not this lovely lady now in more than difficult straits.

"We don't know how many animals we will find,

April, but what we do find need to be driven to market and it will take more than me and Dog to do that. Do you and Rufus have any friends you can get help from? Even a few teenage boys would do."

"Papa doesn't have a friend in the world," Geneva said. She was coming close to tears, and at twelve years, was fully understanding the difficulties of the moment. "He is just so mean to people. I'm sorry, Mama, for talking like that, but it's true, isn't it?"

"I'm afraid so," April said. "He demands some kind of perfection that he isn't capable of himself, then drives off those he's hired. I can't think of a single person in this valley who would come to his help right now."

Dog-man and Snake were now sitting at the breakfast table with two crying women. Even Terry and Hank had quit their shenanigans and were standing on either side of April, sniffling. "We're gonna need that wagon filled with food and equipment enough for two weeks or more," Snake said, looking back and forth to April and Geneva. *They don't have the slightest idea of the trouble they're in. A wife and three kids and the man doesn't take his herd to market for two years? That man needs a good whuppin'.*

"Either you, April, or you, Geneva, will have to drive that wagon every single day. The other will have to learn the ways of a cow, fast, because we'll need another cow man on the trail." Snake shook his head, tried to smile and poured more coffee. *What am I thinking? It ain't gonna happen and they need to know that. I'd like to ride into town right now and shoot Rufus dead for putting his family in this situation.* "Never mind what I just said."

Snake got up from the table, his breakfast just half eaten and getting cold. He swirled his coffee in the cup and drained it. He paced around the table, touched April lightly on the shoulder, brushed Geneva's hair back some, took a punch at Hank, and sat back down. "Can't be done, April. Gotta face it, Rufus has set this place up to fail. We'll ride out and find as many of your steers and heifers as we can and bring 'em back here, but two cow men can't drive a herd for two weeks across this desert."

"I'm not going to lose my home, Snake," April said. Tears were coursing their way down her face and she squeezed Geneva tight. "Geneva rides far better than I and you have several days to teach her what needs to be taught for the drive. She can ride out with you every day while you bring the herd in. I'll keep you fed and strong."

Determination in a lost cause is what went through Snake's mind as he sat listening. Dog-man looked at Snake and had the same thought. *Snake's gonna do this sure as I'm sittin' here. Them two women are crying and Snake's a gonner.*

"I'm in no position to tell you no, but if I was, that's what I'd say." Snake poured another cup of coffee. "People get bad hurt, even killed, moving cattle, April. We might be fighting off Indians, too. I can't bring that pretty little girl out into that every day." Dog-Man could see it in his eyes. Snake already made up his mind that Geneva would be a drover by the end of the week. He did his best to hold in a chuckle, or maybe it was a snicker.

"Isn't your decision, Mr. Snake," Geneva said. She hugged her mother and stepped back from the table. "It's my ranch, too. If we don't do anything we're gonna lose the ranch. If we try and fail, we're gonna lose the ranch. But, Mr. Snake, if we try and it works, we won't lose the ranch. You think I'm just a girl who's gonna get in the way, but you're wrong. I'm a ranch girl and we're gonna win."

Snake couldn't keep the smile off his face, but the worry in his eyes told the real story. *She's got more gumption at twelve than her father does. Well, we signed on, I guess we ride for this brand now.*

"Then quit talking and get in your working clothes and join us at the corrals," Dog-man said. He got up from the table and walked right out the door, leaving Snake and April to watch him go.

"Best move, girl," Snake said. He nodded to April and followed Dog-man out.

***

"You sit on a horse good," Snake said. "Where would we go to find the nearest water? Cattle, horses, most animals can smell water and will make up camp close to it. Probably find parts of your herd at various water holes."

Geneva pointed off northeast and they rode at a comfortable walk some three miles to a muddy water hole. There were fifteen or so head nearby. "Dog-man, take that left side. Me and Geneva will take the right. Pay attention to what we're doing, girl and learn fast."

They circled well around the cattle and slowly crowded them into getting up and moving. "Watch for one of those older heifers to become a leader and the others will follow along. We don't need to hurry them, just keep them moving back to the ranch. I want you to ride at the back end of this group. Me and Dog will be on each side. Just keep 'em walkin'."

He showed her how to move back and forth, how to chase down one if it tried to escape and was amazed at how fast she learned and how good a rider she was. *I really don't think either she or her mother have the strength to do this every day, all day, for two weeks. They got a lot to lose so maybe that'll give 'em strength.*

At the end of the day they had found three small groups of cattle and the home corrals housed about fifty head. There was only one incident, when they had to cross some water deep in an arroyo and an older heifer found herself mired in mud. Snake put a rope on her as did Dog-man and yelled to Geneva to haze the cow some. Her horse almost got mired in, too. It bucked, jumped and danced some, but the girl rode it out fine. It was the commotion that gave the cow more reason to get out that got her kicking, too.

"We got another problem, Snake," Dog-man said. "Most of this year's crop ain't branded. They've been cut, but not branded. Why would Theron take the time to sort them out and cut them but not brand them? Sure can't take unbranded cattle to the sale yards."

They put their horses up and headed for the well to wash half a ton of desert dust away. "After a day of moving beef, Geneva, you gotta swagger some when you head for the cook wagon. Like this," Snake said, giving a little Texas two-step toward the wash trough.

Almost so tired she could have slept while walking, Geneva gave it her best, the smile working its way through the caked dirt on her face. "All right, girl. You got it. You are now one first-class drover and don't let nobody say different." Snake kicked some dirt, Geneva did too, and, all cleaned up, they marched into the kitchen.

"Got three first-class drovers ready for evening meal, Ma'am," Dog-man said. "Best hurry with the little one's, though. She might go to sleep in her plate."

Supper was quick, good, and it took just the hint of bed-time for Geneva to head for bed. "You look like you have a problem, Dog-man." April said. "With Geneva?"

"My, God, no. That girl's got spunk to spare. No. We found that most of the steers that we would be taking to market haven't been branded. Sale yard won't take unbranded cattle. Some of those steers are way past having a high market value, too." What Dog-man wanted to say was something along the lines of Rufus Theron not being much of a cattle rancher. Instead, he said that the herd had been neglected to the point that it didn't have the market value she believed it had.

"Not sure what we're bringing in will make your land payments. If we can find good numbers of beef in the next several days, like we did today, I hope we will have time to brand before we start out for Gila Bend."

So many problems, just one after another. I'm not strong enough for this. April wiped away a tear and looked deep into Dog-man's sad face. *Why, Rufus? Why couldn't you just do your job and let the hired hands do theirs? I can't quit, not now, not with Geneva giving everything that little girl has to give.* She held in her sobs until Snake and Dog-man headed for the bunkhouse and then laid her head on the dining room table and cried for a solid hour.

April sat straight up, ran her hands through her long hair, and got to her feet. *That's it. No more crying, no more feeling sorry for myself. Rufus got us into this, but it will be me getting us through it. My mother did it in Missouri, by damn I can do it here.* April was Geneva's age when her father was killed in a tornado and their house and barn was destroyed. "Mama refused to accept defeat and by damn so will I," she muttered.

10

Major Fleming walked into Doctor McCarthy's office. He'd heard rumors and wanted to get the full story from the doctor. Fleming was sure the Therons would never be able to make their payment and needed to be ready to take over the ranch. It was good property, had good water, and would be an easy re-sale.

Lovely April and the children will suffer a bit, but it would be just a short time before she found another man. She knew what a failure Rufus was when she married the fool. "Rufus able to have a visitor, Doc?"

"Take him with you when you leave, for all I care, Major. Biggest pain I've had in a long time. Man doesn't have genial bone in his body."

Elmer Spaulding, the doctor's aide, cook, housekeeper and friend walked in. "Hello Major." Spaulding turned to Doctor McCarthy. "He's not responding to anything."

"What's his situation? I've heard rumors of him losing his leg. That true?"

"Afraid so," McCarthy said. "Took it off yesterday. Arrow was covered with filthy stuff and gangrene took over. Don't know what else they might have dipped that blade into. He's got a bad fever, can't keep food down and might just kick off on me." The doctor walked over and opened the door to Theron's room and nodded to the major.

"Don't understand a man being that angry at the world all day every day," The doctor said. "Blames everyone around him for his problems and can't comprehend that he brings them on himself. I feel bad about April and those children. They're gonna be without a man or a home, aren't they." It was a statement, not a question.

"That's what I'm here to talk to him about, Doc. See if I can pound some sense through that thick skull of his." Major Fleming was escorted into Theron's bedroom and they found him unconscious and with a high fever. He was babbling about Indians, fire and strangers getting fresh with his daughter.

A one-legged man can't run a ranch and he's already behind in his payments. If I can get him to sign off on our contract, sign the deed over to me, I can sell it quick. I sometimes think I enjoy working with these stupid people. They make it so easy to make money.

"Wake up, Rufus. Wake up." Fleming shook Theron hard, but the wounded man didn't respond, just kept murmuring nonsense. "I've got a buyer for your place, Theron, a way out for you, with enough left over to give you a start somewhere else. Wake up, damn it."

McCarthy moved Fleming aside and sat down next to Rufus. He wiped the feverish man's forehead with a damp cloth, pried an eye open, tried to smell his breath and shook his head. "He's got bad fever, infection inside, I'm afraid. I can't save him, Major."

Fleming thanked the doctor and went out to his buggy. "I better ride out to the Theron place and have a long talk with April. This ain't gonna be as easy as it would have been." He had told Rufus he had a buyer, but of course that was a lie. He'd foreclose and get the lot of them off the property and then find a buyer.

It won't work that way with April. I'll have to offer her some way out that won't jeopardize the children. If he was working with Rufus, he'd simply foreclose, take all the cattle and equipment at well below market value and in the end own the herd, land and equipment, making no payment to Rufus. *Well, I've got fifteen miles to come up with a good plan.*

***

"There may still be a few critters out there, April, but we can't take any more time to find them. We're fighting time right now." Snake was standing at the gate to a fenced pasture filled with slightly more than two hundred and fifty steers. "The older ones haven't fared well, I'm afraid. Hide buyers will take them, not meat buyers and that means much lower prices."

April's red-rimmed eyes told Snake what he already knew. Disaster for what was left of the Theron family. "Major Fleming will demand full payment following the fall sales and I won't have it. Rufus won't be able to work for months and we won't have anywhere to live. What am I gonna do, Snake?"

"I wish I had an answer for you." Snake could feel anger welling up from deep in his soul, the same anger he felt when Sloan made his moves on Mercy Potter. When ugly and bad things happen to good people, Snake was the kind of man who simply couldn't stand by and watch. "I gotta have a talk with Dog-man, April. We'll start the branding later today. We'll need you and Geneva in the corrals with us."

"Branding? I've never done any branding, Snake."

"I know. Neither had I the first time." He smiled, tipped his hat, and headed for a long talk with Dog-man. She stood in wonder, watching him saunter across the open yard.

***

"Got that flask of yours handy, Dog? Heap big talk-time, partner."

"What have you done?" Dog-man could smell trouble, rustled around in his saddlebags and found a flask of whiskey. "How much is it gonna hurt?"

"Some, maybe," Snake said. He took a long slug of hot whiskey and sat down in the dirt, his back on a fence post. "We been ridin' with that girl for a week, got two weeks on the trail lookin' us in the eye and I ain't willing to let those women lose this ranch." Snake rarely talked fast, but he was shoving those words out quick.

"Don't know what their land payment is, but I'm thinkin', and I don't want you to get all riled on this, but I'm thinkin' we should just make their payment, help them get a good herd started, find them a good ranch foreman and move on to San Diego." He eased some more whiskey down his throat, gave a sideways glance at Dog-man, expecting to see a fist flying at him.

"Been thinkin' the same thing, Snake. Her old man ain't gonna be worth nothin' if he even heals up. She needs a ranch foreman first and there ain't one locally or he would have already been here. Got something worked out, do you?"

"You're right and nope, I don't. Think you and the family can work the branding fires tomorrow? Thinking of visiting Puny Russell."

"I'm good with women and children, Snake. Sure, old man, just ride on off to Tucson." Snake ignored the jibe, smiled and took another long drink of whiskey.

***

April found herself standing alone, inside the pasture laughing softly. *Why couldn't I have found a man like him.* She undid the gate and walked out, making sure it was closed tight. She found Geneva at the wash trough, wiping mud from her face. "Looks like you drovers found all our cattle."

"Hi, Mama. Eight days straight I've been on the back of a horse eating dirt. Snake says we only have a few days to get them branded and then it's off to Gila Bend. You want to know something?"

"All right, what?"

"I'm going to find a man just like Snake and marry him, that's what."

April tightened up just a bit, thinking that's what she should have done, too. "Good for you, honey. We have to be prepared to lose this place, though. Snake doesn't think we'll make enough money at the sale to make our payment. It's time again for you and me to be tough and strong. I'll fight it to the end, but we have to be prepared for the worst."

"I don't like it when we talk like this, Mama. Don't. Maybe later. I have to help Dog-man and Snake set up for the branding. I talked with Dog-man and he said that Hank and Terry can help with the fire and the irons."

"You know what we're going to be doing? I've never even seen Rufe brand."

"We've been talking about it for several days, Mama. Let's walk over to the corrals and I'll explain the whole thing for you. Did you and Pa talk about the herd much? Dog-man has asked me questions about the cattle that I can't answer."

"What kind of questions, honey?"

"Well, like, why have the steers been cut but not branded and why wasn't there a drive to market last year? I had to say I don't know. Do you?"

April had been worrying when these questions from the children would start. Why wasn't their father doing the right things around the ranch? Why didn't hired hands stick around for more than a week or two at best? Why wasn't the stew pot always full or why didn't they have new clothing from time to time?

"This probably isn't the best time to talk about this, Geneva, but I'm afraid we have to. I'll simply put it bluntly to you, honey. Your father isn't the man he thinks he is. He's mean with people, sometimes even his own family. That's mostly why we can't keep good hands. There's a lot more to it, Geneva, but you're smarter than most, you can figure it out."

Geneva saw the tears running down her mother's cheeks, heard the tremble in her voice, and knew many of the answers immediately. "I'm sorry, Mama." They walked toward where Snake and Dog-man were talking with Hank and Terry.

"Looks like you've got company coming, April." Snake was pointing at dust out on the roadway. "Better run for the rifles, Dog-man. At least we know whoever it is ain't Indian. Come in behind the fence, April, Geneva and we'll wait for 'em."

Dog-man sprinted to the bunkhouse and returned with two rifles and boxes of cartridges. "Recognize him?" There was just the buggy driver and a fine team coming at a comfortable trot.

"Yes," April said. "It's Major Fleming. He has the loan on the property. Oh, dear. Rufus said he gave us an extension until after the sale. I hope that wasn't a lie. Stay with me, Snake, when he gets here. Please."

"We will." Snake went out of his way to include Dog-man. "Let's walk back toward the house. Geneva, can you keep the boys occupied for a while? We need those fires laid out and the branding irons cleaned up."

"I'd sure rather be with you and Mama, but I'll do it," she said. For her age she could read developing problems far better than most of those who are fully grown. She kicked some dirt and yelled at her brothers to join her in the barn.

***

"Hello, Major. What brings you out this way?" April did her best to offer a smile. Snake was on one side and Dog-man on the other, both carrying rifles. "Come in. I'll get some coffee brewing."

"Take my horses, son," Major Fleming said. He stepped down from the buggy and reached for April's hand.

"Ain't your son, Mister." Snake stepped between them and April put her hand on Snake's arm, walking toward the house. "I'll get the door, April."

Dog-man stifled a chuckle as best he could, took the lead rope from Fleming and tied off the team. "I got 'em, old man. These trotters will be fine right here. Think they could use some water on a fine day like this?"

Dog-man dipped his head ever so slightly, Major Fleming growled and they followed Snake and April into the kitchen. "Coffee coming up," she said. "Grab a chair, gentlemen and be comfortable. Geneva baked some fresh bread and there's jam in the jar."

"Who are these men, April?" Fleming was glaring at the drovers as he took a chair.

"I'm Snake and this here is Dog-man," Snake said. "Nice to meet you."

"Humph," Fleming said. "A couple of saddle tramps looking to take your ranch, April? Want me to notify the sheriff?"

April caught the drift from Snake's attitude and, just as Geneva would have done, said, "Snake's my ranch foreman, Major, and Dog-man's my new cow-boss. We'll be trailing the herd to Gila Bend in just a few days. Could use another hand if you can build a loop."

Snake guffawed, slapped Dog-man on the shoulder and stuck a hand, out to Fleming. "By gawd you're right, April. We could use another good hand. What say you?"

"Enough nonsense," Fleming snarled. "I'm here

to discuss business with Mrs. Theron. Now, if you two will excuse us, please."

"No, Major," April said. "I want them right where they are. For you to come out here at this time, means you know something I don't. Either about our loan or about Rufus. Which is it?" She had the coffee on the stove and was standing with her hands on her thin hips. *No matter what he says I'm not going to cry, not going to breakdown. Enough is enough.* She looked at Snake, then back to Fleming.

That's the tough I've been waiting for. Snake had a smile on his face, sat forward in his chair and dipped some jam for his bread. *She's gonna be fine.*

"Actually, it's about Rufus," Fleming said. He glared at Snake and Dog-man and turned his attention to April. "Doc McCarthy had to take Rufus's leg, April. He'll never ranch again. That's why I'm here. To offer my sympathy and to make what I think is a generous offer on the property."

April sagged into a chair, tears running down her cheeks. "That's terrible. Poor Rufe. He'll never be able to work the ranch having just one leg." She stood up, blew her nose, and brought the coffee pot to the men. She started to say something when Geneva rushed in.

"More dust coming," She said, pointing out toward Tucson. "Single rider."

Dog-man was out the door with his rifle and watched Elmer Spaulding ride in. "Know him?" Dog-Man asked.

"It's Mr. Spaulding from the doctor's," Geneva said. "What did Major Fleming have to say?"

"I'm sure we'll discuss all that real soon, little one." Dog-man said. He moved back a step or two and took a good look at this Mr. Spaulding. He stood well over six feet and had to weigh more than two-twenty-five. Spaulding was wearing a sheer white shirt and his almost black arms, shoulder,s and chest muscles rippled in the sunlight.

"Hi, Mr. Spaulding," Geneva said. "This is Dog-man and his friend Mr. Snake is inside with mama and Major Fleming."

"You look like you've been working in the sun, my lady," Spaulding said. He smiled and nodded to Dog-man. "Looking mighty healthy."

Dog-man took the reins from Spaulding and Geneva led the big man into the kitchen.

"Hello, April," Spaulding said. "I'm afraid I'm bringing some bad news." Spaulding filled the kitchen. His broad face was a deep shade of brown and his head carried long black hair that hung, wind-blown, in waves and loose curls. His mother was the daughter of a run-away slave who married a French card-shark in New Orleans and his father was a Boston ship's captain who beached himself on the Texas coast thirty years ago. Spaulding spoke in a deep voice that seemed to fill any room he was in.

His size would intimidate most but it was the lines trailing out from his eyes that gave the man away. Some call them crow's feet, many call them laugh lines, and humor was writ large in Spaulding's eyes and face. Those eyes also seemed filled with sadness, though, as he spoke to April.

"Major Fleming just told me about Rufus's leg, Elmer, but thank you for coming out."

"No, Ma'am," Spaulding said. "I'm afraid it's worse. Mr. Theron didn't survive taking the arrow out. He passed earlier today. I know how difficult it will be and I want you to know that I'm here for whatever you might need."

"I'm hoping Mrs. Theron won't need anything more than help moving off the ranch," Fleming said. There was a forced smile but not in his eyes. There was no offering of condolence, either. The banker was there, purely for business.

"Rufus said you had given him an extension until we sold the herd in Gila Bend," April said. "Has that been withdrawn?" Her attitude was that of a strong woman, not the weepy one Fleming was expecting. "We'll be driving the herd to Gila Bend, Major, after which, I plan to make up our two late payments. This ranch is not for sale."

Fleming sat quietly for just a moment. "Yes, I did give Rufus an extension, but I hardly believe these two saddle-tramps can get the herd to Gila Bend. You have exactly one month, April, to make those two payments or I'll be forced to foreclose." He got up, bowed to the lady, and strode from the kitchen. Dog-man and Elmer Spaulding followed, Snake stayed with April and Geneva.

"Need help untethering those chargers, old man?" Dog-man watched Fleming fight with the lead rope. "Don't get your fingers all rough and red, now."

"Get out of my way," Fleming said, grabbing up the rope. He got in the carriage and drove out of the yard.

"Not a nice man," Elmer said. "Do you really think you can save the lady's ranch? Old man Theron was never right with the people he hired, but he has the nicest family. Understand it was you and Snake that chased off the attackers. Mr. Theron wasn't the right kind of person to run a ranch like

this. He didn't like anyone, couldn't bring himself
to work with those he hired, and wouldn't listen to
those who were successful." Spaulding wiped his
brow and followed Dog-man up the porch stairs.
"What are your plans?"

"Let's go back inside and we'll spell it out for
you. Gonna be about the strangest drive I've ever
been on."

11

"Incredible." Elmer Spaulding's eyes were almost shiny listening to Snake outline how they would get the branding done and make the long, two-week drive to Gila Bend. "I've been to that sale more than once and most of the cattle that are brought in are in good shape. You might not come out well, April."

"I'm not losing this place without a fight. A big fight," April said.

"You work for Doctor McCarthy and go to stock sales in Gila Bend?" Snake's curiosity was shared by the others sitting around the kitchen table.

"Doc has a ranch in this valley, as well, Snake and I've bought some fine replacement heifers and bulls at that stockyard. I've even ridden a time or two with the drovers taking Doc's herd to the sale. It's quite a show, I'm telling you."

"Ever consider leaving Doctor McCarthy's employ, Mr. Spaulding?" Dog-man had been mesmerized by the man from first sight and hoped he would join their trail drive. "Me and Snake and Geneva are the drovers so far and we could use another man with trail experience." Dog-man looked first at Snake, then at April who beamed.

"Wonderful idea, Dog-man. Oh, Elmer," she cried, "What a wonderful idea. Would Doc let you go for that long?" She caught herself. "I'm sorry. You haven't answered and I'm already packing your trail kit." She was blushing and Geneva giggled.

"Gotcha outnumbered, Spaulding. Might not let you out until you say yes," Snake laughed.

"Then," he stood up and pretended to cower some. "Tender, helpless little me better say yes. Three big boys, one big girl and those beeves are going to move right along. Be a good time to teach Hank the better part of cattle ranching."

"Hank's too young," April said.

"He's ten, April." Spaulding gave her a quick wink. "Half a man already. Needs to earn his way in this tough old life."

That seemed to end the conversation and like it or not, Hank was about to learn the ways of the trail hand. They spent what was left of the day planning out the final two days of branding and the long drive. "Won't need a full two weeks of food, April," Elmer said. "There's a couple of villages along the way. Never found Indians to be trouble, but some of the locals seem to always need a steer or two and can be aggressive.

"I'll go pack up and be here at first light for branding." Spaulding took April's hand and squeezed it, gently. "We'll give it the biggest fight possible, April. I'm so sorry for your loss."

***

Terry was in charge off keeping the fires going, Snake and Dog-man were roping the steers, Elmer and April were holding them down and Geneva and Hank were running the branding irons. Hank learned the hard way why gloves were necessary, Terry got splinters on every load of wood and Dog-man ran out of patience first. The first hour was chaos, but things began to fall into place quickly.

"Gonna be the longest two weeks of our lives, Snake. I ain't never heard such squallin' as that Terry and his splinters. Are we gonna hear that every day?"

"You ain't seen my fun partner anywhere, have you, stranger?" Snake was looking up and down, back and forth and Dog-man finally broke down and laughed. "There he is," Snake laughed. "Thought he'd left the territory."

"Thank you, partner," Dog-Man said. "With everything that's gone wrong, we've branded a lot of cattle this morning. Having Elmer on the crew made a big difference. Hank and Terry are gonna be fine as our camp boys, but we need to get Hank in the saddle a few times before we leave. He's young, doesn't pay that much attention, but we might need him along the way."

"April tends to keep him away from chores and the like. I'll talk to her. Let's bust this up and have something to eat."

They needed someone to move the branded cattle out of the working pen and that person didn't exist. At noon meal, they used the branding fires to heat a kettle of stew and ate in the shade of the barn, drinking gallons of water. "Are we even making progress?" April asked. "There are just as many cattle in that pen as when we started."

"Me and Dog will do some sorting before we start up again. Hey, Hank, you ride a horse, do you?"

"Papa says I'm too stupid to ride horses," he said, tears coming to the surface in quantity. He jumped to his feet and ran to the house. April tried to get up and follow and Snake told her to sit still.

"I'll take care of this," Snake said. "Is that why he isn't allowed to do chores and the like?"

"Rufus says he's slow, Snake. Says he'll never be able to do a man's chores."

"Well, hell, woman, what so you think he's been doing all morning long."

Snake was getting riled and Dog-man jumped in before too much more was said. "He's right, April. They ain't nothing wrong with that boy ceptin' he ain't allowed to do nothing. You go have a talk with Hank, Snake. I think it's time that boy is allowed to be a young man."

April looked back and forth at the two men wondering just how and why they ended up on this ranch. *Rufus would never let Hank be a boy, be his son and expected absolute perfection. And along comes Snake and Dog-man who want Hank to be a boy. I've got a lot to learn.*

Dog-man re-filled his bowl with stew and sat down next to April. "I'm terribly sorry you lost your husband, April, but you got to know by now that he weren't much of a rancher or father. You've got three wonderful kids and they've worked their little hind ends off this morning, not to mention their mother, too."

"Papa would never let Hank ride a horse," Geneva said. "But I've been teaching him how. He isn't as strong as I am, but he can ride."

"He'll be strong when these next few weeks are over," Dog-man said. "Are you all right with how things are moving along, April? Today is an example of what life on the trail is going to be like."

"Rufus changed so much when Hank was born. I don't know why. For all these years, the ranch has gone downhill, our marriage slipped away and I let it happen. I'm a much stronger woman than what you've seen, Dog-man. Rufe had us all believing that Hank was backward, but it was Rufe constantly berating the boy that made it seem so." She fought off the tears by getting to her feet and gathering up the dinner bowls.

I am not going to cry one more time because of that man. My children are going to be as tough as Snake and Dog-man, and I'm going to make this ranch work. I am. April called Geneva over and the two of them washed off the plates. "I want you to help Hank learn how to be a big tough boy. Can you do that? You're a charming and lovely young lady, but you're also tougher than most boys I know and Hank needs to know how to be like that."

"Papa said nasty things about Hank and Terry, made them cry all the time. Hank is afraid of just about everything. He did really good this morning. Those branding irons are hot and heavy, but he did good, even after he burned his hands."

***

"Well, son, if what I saw you doing this morning is being backward, I guess you're about the best at it. Darn good work out there, Hank." Snake was sitting on the edge of the bed where Hank had run to. "You didn't answer my question. Do you ride?"

"Geneva has been trying to teach me, but I think I'm too backward to learn good," he said. The sobs came again and the boy buried his head in a pillow. "It's fun to ride a horse. Papa would have beat me bad if he had caught us. Geneva, too."

Snake felt the anger boiling up, hearing about the children being beat by Rufus Theron. *That man's lucky he's dead. Beat your children? Call them backward to their face? Something this boy needs to get out of his head.* "When we finish our branding later today, how about you and me going for a ride out into the desert?"

"Really? Yes, Snake, yes." The boy cried it out, threw his arms around the tall man, and wiped away the tears. "I'll show you I'm not backward. Geneva knows it, too."

"I'll bet she does, Pard. Let's go to work. Got calves to brand, dust to kick." Hank had a strong hold of Snake's hand as they walked back to the branding pens. Dog-man and April watched the two do a little two-step going through the gate. "Kick some dust, Pard. It makes you feel better." Hank was laughing loud, kicking dirt in every direction, right along with Snake.

12

"Always keep your back straight, have some weight in your stirrups, and feel balanced with your horse," Snake said. "Don't ride the saddle, ride the horse." Dog-man couldn't hold in the laugh. This was the man who literally lounged in the saddle when he rode. Laid back, one elbow on the horses rump sometimes, calling for Hank to ride in balance with his horse.

"That's fine son," Snake said. "You look good. Let's step them up a little and feel the rhythm of the horse." They moved into a gentle trot and Hank grabbed hold of the saddle horn. "No, you don't need to hold on to nothin'," Snake said. "See how the rhythm feels?" Hank had the reins pulled up some and Snake told him to give them some freedom. "That's it. Keep a light touch on the reins so that when you want the horse to do something, he'll know it."

It wasn't an hour and the boy was riding at a solid lope alongside Snake, laughing and whooping at the top of his lungs. Dog-man, Geneva, April, and Elmer were following as they rode back into the yard at the ranch. Snake and Hank jumped from the horses and kicked some dust.

"I did good, Snake. I did good." The boy was beside himself, almost dancing in his joy. Snake couldn't hide his smile and helped getting all the saddles off and on their racks. "Did you see me, Mama? Snake's gonna teach me how to move cattle, too. I'm not backward, am I?"

"You never were, Hank. You never were."

***

"How many more need branding?" Snake and Elmer were finishing moving the branded cattle in to the holding pens on the second day.

"I think we got 'em," Elmer said. "Got the steers in this pen, all branded and the cull heifers in that pen. Looks like about a hundred and fifty-two steers and twenty-seven culls. Make for a nice herd to move. There's good water from here to Gila Bend, nothing too steep for us to cross."

"Good," Snake said. "Let's get the wagon packed, make sure we have our bed rolls, slickers, guns and ammunition, and extra clothing for everyone. April and Geneva are getting the food and kitchen ready for packing, too. Leave at the crack of dawn and we'll be one day ahead of our schedule."

"Hank has become a good little rider Elmer, but we'll have to watch him close when we're with the cattle. Geneva will do fine. She's been bringing the strays in with me for several days. I think we'll do fine once we get moving."

"We'll need to trade off on night riding, Snake.

That's when the local raiders hit the herds coming through. They sneak in and take three, four, maybe more, late at night. If we were on one of those long Texas drives, the kids could do the night riding, but here, we won't just be keeping the herd in order, we'll be fighting raiding parties."

"No mercy on those that try to steal April's cattle, my friend. Shoot 'em on sight would be my answer."

"And mine," Spaulding said. "I'm hungry as a bear. Hope April's Dutch oven is full tonight, cuz I'm gonna empty it."

***

One could almost feel the electricity as they filtered into the kitchen well before sunrise. April was cooking stacks of hotcakes, Geneva was bringing trays of hot biscuits from the oven, and the coffee pot was never empty.

"It's during these first hours that the herd will be a bit difficult. They don't know the plan yet," Snake said. "Dog-man, you lead and we'll probably find our lead cow quickly. Calves love to try and run off, so Elmer, you and Geneva work the sides. Me and Hank will ride drag today. You be all right with Terry in the wagon, April?"

"We'll be fine, Snake. I'm so excited I'll want to run that team, but I know I can't. Did you thank Doctor McCarthy for the sack of beans and the box of onions, Elmer? What a gentleman."

"Yes, Ma'am, I did. We've got dried and smoked meat and a barrel of salt meat, too. Won't be having to get extra food at the little villages on the way, so might get missed by some of the trail raiders."

"Ain't nothing more to talk about, ain't nothing more to eat on the table, let's move 'em out, then. Got sunlight shining on us shortly." Snake was as excited as April and her kids and got the crew moving toward the door. In less than half an hour, Dog-man in the lead, Elmer and Geneva started moving the cattle out.

Snake stood tall in the stirrups and watched the herd line out, saw Geneva catch a get-away and Elmer bring a couple back, too. He had fleeting thoughts of the screaming Potter children, so mis-behaved that even the softest hearted of those on the train scorned them. Thought of the always angry Mercy Potter and her treatment of her husband and wondered how it was that he was happy being with April and her children.

"Two families from different worlds," he murmured. He and Hank worked the drag, kept the herd moving right along, and Snake tried not to think of April and the kids. Couldn't. "Dammit," he muttered. "We're gonna save that ranch for her and then what?"

His thoughts wouldn't go away. Could she and Geneva really run that ranch? Could she find a real cow man for a foreman? What would she pay him with? *She needs a husband, but with a run-down ranch and three kids, she ain't likely to find one.* The possibility of Snake being that husband never entered his mind.

"How much further?" Hank was covered in dust but smiling ear to ear.

"About two weeks farther to go, Hank. Did you put some biscuits and smoked meat in your saddle-bags like I said?"

"Sure did," he said. "That's what I meant. How much further till we stop and eat? I'm hungry." He had been a poor eater when Snake and Dog-man arrived at the ranch but working the branding pens and riding a horse every day lit off the boy's appetite.

"We've only been out for an hour or so, Hank. Another couple of hours and we can dig in." *I ain't never much cared one way or the other about kids. How come it seems I have two of 'em all at once? Dog-man's been on me about how April comes to me for anything she needs, and how the kids do the same.* He growled something that Hank didn't understand and rode to his left to move one of the slower calves along.

"Don't want to be thinkin' like this, Snake. No I don't." He didn't even try to hide his smile, partially hidden by a covering of sweated dust.

***

"Did only about eight miles, Dog. Gotta do better if we're gonna make that sale. Herd's been learnin' good and all of us done good, too. Just need to pick it up tomorrow. I'll be night rider tonight. April, you and the kids sleep under the wagon and you keep those rifles of yours handy. Dog, you and Elmer sleep out and away from the fire with your rifles. Don't be shootin' me if I ride in for some coffee."

"Got it covered, Snake," Elmer said. "We were watched when we lit out. More than likely Major Fleming's boys keeping track. He wants that ranch of yours, April, but I don't think he's a threat to the herd."

"Of course he is," she said. She was shaking her

head, angry at the thought of the man. "If I can't get these dumb old cows to Gila Bend, I can't make those payments I promised. He's a threat, Elmer and he's just nasty enough to try something like running them off during the night."

"That's all he'd have to do," Snake said. "Not steal any, just run 'em off. Take us time to round 'em back up and after a time or two, we wouldn't make the sale. All off that means we better be on high alert. I'm off now. Get some sleep." He stepped into the saddle and rode off into a blazing sunset.

Hank was the first to find his bedroll, followed in order by Geneva and April. Dog-man and Elmer settled down by the fire with a flask of brandy. "Snake's out with the herd, I'm thinkin' maybe I'll take a little ride back along the trail and see what I can see," Dog-man said. "Could use some backup and company. Shouldn't take us just a few minutes to see if we are being followed."

"Be no other reason for a campfire," Elmer chuckled. They put some fresh wood on the fire and saddled their horses. The ride back along the trail was an easy one, but when they rode across the top of a hump in the ground, they spotted the fire, less than a half a mile away.

Both men were off their horses and back on the other side of the rise. "We were silhouetted, Elmer. Hope we weren't seen. Think we should get closer?" Dog-man asked. "Anybody looking at that sunset would have seen us."

"It would be nice to know how many are working against us. Wait another half an hour and it'll be dark enough to move over the rise. Think outlaws look at sunsets?"

"Don't know," Dog-man said. "Ain't never been an outlaw."

It was a quick half hour and the two walked their horses over the rise and didn't mount until they were in the hollow below. They rode easy and slow to a stand of trees in another little hollow. "We'll just ease up to the lip and take a quick look," Elmer said.

"Five of 'em," Dog-man whispered. "Ain't that Fleming on the right there?"

"'Tis indeed. Better get back. Quiet now."

They eased their way out of the hollow, mounted and walked their horses for at least half a mile before trotting the rest of the way into camp. "I'm gonna find Snake and tell him what we found," Dog-man said. "Better wake April. She needs to know. They'll probably hit the herd tonight."

"I'll join you and Snake as soon as I get April and the kids up. They've fought off Indians, they can fight off outlaws," Elmer's chuckle was more of a deep purr, as a tiger might make.

***

"Important to remember, men. I don't want Mrs. Theron or those children injured." Major Fleming was sipping a cup of whiskey and chewing on a cigar. "Scatter those steers across half the territory and have fun doing it, but don't hurt that family."

"What about the men she hired for the drive?" One of Fleming's raiders asked.

"Kill 'em, wound 'em, run 'em. off. Do whatever needs to be done, but get that herd scattered. Mrs. Theron is not going to get that herd into Gila Bend, is not going to make her land payment. Now, mount up men and ride hard. If, somehow, you are caught, you do not work for me. You were just out trying to catch a range cow to feed your wife and kids."

There was general laughter from the group as they stepped into their saddles for the night's work. It was a quiet ride for the two miles to the herd and the men kept close watch for anyone who might be out and about. "There's water and grass about half a mile west, boys. Watch for a night rider. Best bet is to ride in hard, yelling at the top of our lungs and firing our pistols. Maybe we can make it sound like an Indian raid."

The four riders spread out a little and moved toward the water hole. "There," one of them said. He was pointing at a lone rider some hundred yards or so in front of them.

"As soon as we know exactly where the cattle are, we'll attack. Shoot that rider first," the leader said. They advanced slowly across the open desert and topped a small knoll that gave them a good view of the herd standing around the water hole. Before the leader could start the charge, a shot rang out and one of the raiders howled in pain as he fell from his horse.

The lone night rider and two of his friends came at a full gallop toward the three remaining raiders, guns blazing. The leader fell with a bullet through his head and the other two raced as hard as they could into the dark night.

"Enough," Snake yelled. "Get back to the herd and let's hope our gunfire didn't kick 'em off." Snake led them back and they found the herd moving about some, but too tired from the first day's drive to want to run. "Let's find those two who fell. Maybe at least one might be alive."

One was alive and Dog-man had him propped up against a fallen log near the fire. Snake and Elmer stayed with the herd just in case of another attack. "You ever seen this gentleman before, April? He took a bullet in his chest and might not be with us much longer."

"He works for Mr. Harrington at the black-smith's," Geneva said. "Cleans the stalls and feeds. He's not a nice man. Says nasty things to people."

"He rode in the company that Major Fleming formed to fight the Indians, too," April said. "According to Doctor McCarthy he spent most of his time hoisting a bottle instead of fighting."

"Didn't fight much tonight, either," Dog-man said. "Me and Elmer found Fleming and four men at their camp and it was four men came to scatter the herd. Fleming only has two now. Don't know if that means the end of his attempts or not, but we better stay alert for the next few days."

"He wants my ranch, Dog-man. Badly. I think it's because we have such good water and grass. Rufus bought the place in a government sale, but Fleming ended up with the mortgage papers and he's been after Rufe from day one. He's not running me off."

***

The two Fleming Raiders stood, hang-dog like, in front of the fire, listening to Fleming scream obscenities at them. "They attacked you! You were supposed to attack them," he yelled. "Two men dead and no cattle run off? I paid you to do a job and all you did was turn tail and run off."

Fleming paced around, talking, shouting, thinking and sat down near the fire. "Get me my whiskey," he said. "I want you two to continue following Mrs. Theron's herd while I go back to town for more help. They must have been expecting us. Well, expect or not, the next time will be different. I'll bring six men back with me."

He left for town at daybreak and his two men rode behind the Theron herd, staying at least two miles back. "We come close to a village or town, I'm bailing out," the larger of the two said. "I think Mrs. Theron hired some killers to protect that herd and I ain't ready to die for fifty dollars."

"Why wait? Let's just ride north. I ain't got nothing in Tucson that I can't replace. Could use a change of scenery, anyway."

They laughed, shook hands at their new partnership and turned north. "I didn't like the idea of hurting that lady, anyway."

13

"I have never been this tired in my whole life," Hank said. He plopped down in the dirt alongside the fire Geneva put together. It was the end of the fifth day on the trail and they had pushed the herd over the top of a small range of craggy mountains filled with spiny bushes, cactus that reached out for them and little grass or water. "Tell mama I want a whole steer for supper."

Geneva laughed. "I'm so proud of you, Hank. I always knew you weren't backward. Always. What's wrong with your hand?" He was holding his right hand with his left and wincing some as he flexed his finger.

"Caught it in the rope chasing that one steer out of the rocks. It hurts, Geneva."

She sat down next to him and took his hand in hers. "Don't look right, Hank. Better let Snake see that. Finger's twisted wrong. I'll go get him."

Snake was picketing the horses in what little grass was available when Geneva ran up. "Hank's hurt his hand, Snake. One finger is twisted wrong."

"Be right there, girl. Find your ma and we'll get him fixed up." *I wonder if April knows just what a fine bunch of kids she has. That boy's gained ten pounds since we left out and is stronger than any ten-year-old I've ever met. What am I thinking? Except for me, I've never ever seen another ten-year-old.*

He was still chuckling when he found Hank and April by the fire. "Geneva's gone off to bring Dogman and Elmer in for supper," April said. "Looks like he's dislocated a finger, Snake. It's already trying to swell up. I told him putting it back in place might hurt some and he just grinned at me."

Snake laughed and bent down to look at the injury. "That's a rope popper, Hank. Ain't a drover alive ain't done that at least once. Saw a man throw a loop at a yearling, wince when he caught him and when he took his glove off, his thumb stayed in the glove. Rope cut it clean off."

Hank shuddered but didn't cry or moan and it was April who did. "That's horrible, Snake." She said. She started to gather Hank up, but he shook her off and offered his hurt hand to Snake.

Snake knew the best bet was to make this quick, no preliminaries and took Hank's hand with one hand, grasped the hurt finger with the other and jerked hard. Hank squalled loud and long. April gasped and Snake quickly had a rag soaked in cold water wrapped around the boy's fingers. "Keep that rag wet with cold water and he'll be fine, April." Snake ran his fingers through the boy's hair and reached for the coffee pot.

"Where's the rest of the crew?" April was looking all around. It was just the three of them at the fire.

"Should have been in by now."

Terry came running into the camp. "Mama, mama, Geneva's hurt."

The three raced to where Terry was pointing and found Geneva walking her horse in, holding her side and limping. Snake got there in time to catch her. He saw the blood where she was holding her side, picked her up in his arms and headed back for the fire.

"Bring her horse, Hank. April, get clean linen. Terry, get firewood." He eased her down on a bedroll. "What happened, girl?" He moved her hand away from the wound. "My God, she's been stabbed. Geneva, can you talk. What happened?"

"Three men, Snake. Tried to grab me. Knife. Hurts." She passed out as April returned with fresh linen. Snake was cleaning the wound, which had bled quite a bit and applied some salve that April brought. He got the wound wrapped and Geneva inside her bedroll.

"I've got to get out there," Snake said. "Get your rifles when Terry gets in with the wood keep him with you. Something's very wrong." He raced for his horse and got it saddled and bridled and rode hell for leather toward where the herd was bedded. *Three men attacked Geneva? Where is Dog-man and Elmer?* He raced out of the trees in time to see three men riding toward where the herd should be.

He put his horse in a full gallop, had his revolver out, and when he was close enough, started firing as fast as he could cock the heavy single action. He was howling at the top of his lungs and rode right through the three men, slashing back and forth with the gun. Snake circled hard to his left and prepared for a second charge when he saw one man fall from his horse and a second one bent over in great pain.

Seeing Snake coming on hard, the third man turned and raced away and Snake didn't follow. Instead, he rode up next to the wounded man and slammed him in the head with his gun, knocking him to the ground and took the necessary time to reload. Snake rode toward the herd looking for Dog-man and Elmer.

"Where is Dog?" He muttered, standing tall in the stirrups for a better look around. He saw dust at least a mile off but not from the direction his third rider took and loped off toward it. "Better be you, Dog-man, or I'm in trouble," he chuckled. There were three riders coming hard toward him and Snake decided his best bet was to hunker down behind a rock and take 'em on from ground level.

He had the big gun cocked and aimed when he recognized Dog-man. Snake stood up and waved at the riders and they turned toward him and pulled up short. "What's going on? Kilt two men back there and Geneva's been stabbed," Snake yelled as they reined in. "Who you got with you?"

"Puny Russell rode out to warn us that we would be attacked. Looks like he didn't get here in time, eh? You say you killed two? Let's bring 'em into the camp. Puny might know them," Dog-man said.

Snake nodded to Puny, mounted up. They found the two men, one still alive and brought them in. "Geneva was hurt? How bad?" Elmer asked. "Something strange going on, Snake. Something strange."

Terry had a good fire going and April had supper getting hot when they rode in. "I'll take care of the horses," Hank said. He led them off to fair grass and water. He was nursing his sore hand but it didn't slow him down much.

April looked at the wounded man and almost gasped. "It's Henry Babcock from the bank. What happened?"

"Do you know the dead one?" Dog-man asked. She shook her head and turned back to Babcock who was just coming around. He was bleeding from a wound to his right shoulder and from the bash to his head.

"Henry, can you hear me? It's April Theron." He mumbled something no one could understand and looked around at those looking at him. He saw anger and hatred in many faces and slowly closed his eyes. April brought a basin of water and some linen over. "He'll live, Snake. Was he one of the one's who attacked Geneva?"

"It looks that way. How's she doing? That was a nasty wound. You and I need to have a long talk with Puny Russell. Nothing makes much sense right now. Dog-man said Puny rode all the way out here to warn us of an attack just as an attack took place. You up to it, pretty lady?"

"Major Fleming will do anything to keep me from making that sale, Snake. Yes, I'm ready for just about anything. Those men hurt my child. They will know I'm ready, Snake." He saw iron-willed resolve in her normally soft eyes and they walked to where Puny was sitting with Elmer Spaulding.

"Hello, April. Looks like I'm late. I'm sorry," Puny said, jumping to his feet. Seeing his mass standing next to the huge Elmer, Snake almost had to laugh. "Fleming isn't too far behind me. I didn't know about Babcock and his crew."

"Fleming's bringing more?" Dog-man took a quick look at Snake. "Best get back out to the herd, then. He might not wait for dark, this time." He trotted toward the horses and Snake was alongside. "Gonna be another long night, Snake."

"I got an idea." Snake said and stopped running. "Go on out and keep watch on the herd. I think me and Elmer and Puny might just try to ambush us a flim-flam major."

14

"You're all right with this, April?" Snake had outlined his plan to Elmer, April and Puny and everyone nodded at his question. "I'm asking you to be in plenty of danger."

"Yes, you are, Snake." She was smiling and reached for Geneva's hand. "While you men find Major Fleming and put a stop to this, Geneva and I will guard the camp. We're pretty good at it, you know."

"I do know." Snake tousled Geneva's hair smiled at April and nodded to Puny and Elmer. "You got yourself a pretty nasty wound, girl. You gonna be ready for another fight?" Geneva put her hand on her wound but was smiling when she nodded.

"I've been moving around some, just to make sure, Snake. It hurts, but it won't stop me." Her smile was bright, her eyes were bright and Snake just shook his head.

"Best get to moving, then, gents." Snake downed the rest of his coffee. "I gotta ask one more question of you, April. Tell me no if you wish, but I think it's necessary."

"You're going to ask if Hank can ride with Dog-man on the herd, aren't you?" Snake nodded. "It's Hank's herd, too, Snake. He understands the danger. I'll talk to him. You men need to ride out."

This woman is incredible, he thought, walking toward the horses. *Old man Theron never knew the gem he was married to. With Geneva and Hank, and if she can find a decent ranch foreman, she'll have one fine ranch.*

Back trailing along where some 250 cattle walked was easy but watching for the advancing Fleming was difficult. "If we don't spot him first, we'll be riding into an ambush sure as I'm sittin' here," Snake said. "Any ideas?"

"Sun will be setting directly behind us," Elmer said. "We'll have better vision, but I'm wondering if maybe we should spread way apart. A quarter mile between us with you riding in the middle. Might have a better chance of spottin' 'em and not bein' spotted."

"Guess it don't matter none now." Snake drawled it out pointing. "Look at the dust up there." He pointed up the side of a rise, maybe two miles out. "Several men making good time and coming our way. Don't care if they're seen or not. Let's walk our horses over to that rock outcrop and give those boys a good welcome."

"Be dark in half an hour or so," Puny said. "With the sun behind us. Major Fleming ain't gonna like this." The gentle laughter filtered through the late evening's trail dust as the men moved toward a stand of scattered rocks. "I doubt he'll be one of those men coming toward us. He doesn't like to get his hands dirty."

"He won't worry much about his hands when I rub his face in the rocks," Snake growled. "One of his men, a man doing what Fleming told him to do, tried to kill Geneva and no man gets away with that."

There were four riders coming along at a lope and Elmer pointed up the side of a hill at a lone rider. "There's Fleming, I'd bet the barn."

Snake moved back and away from the stand of scattered rocks, found his horse and slowly drifted into a copse of trees, out of sight. Hoping it looked like a loose horse wandering the desert, he moved through the trees and away from Fleming's sight line. "You're mine, Major."

"Just two of us, now," Elmer said. "Let's let 'em get close and open fire. No quarter, but it would be best if we had another prisoner. Attacking a moving herd will get 'em hung for sure."

The riders slowed from a lope to a trot and Elmer looked around to see if something had caused it, or they just wanted to give the horses a breather. "Got that rifle ready?"

"Ready as I'll ever be. Knock one down with the rifle and then go for the Colt," he laughed. "How about you?" He heard a grunt and burrowed into the sand behind the rocks, taking a long quiet bead on the lead rider. His rifle barked at the same time as Elmer's and two men were jerked from their saddles. The other two bailed off their mounts and dashed for cover in a hail of lead.

"Surely should have got one of those others," Puny muttered. "Gettin' old." The huge man snaked his way around the stand of rocks toward where one of the men had ran, saw him dive behind a thorny bunch of brush and sent two rounds into the brush. He heard the grunt, knew at least one of the chunks of lead found a soft home.

Elmer saw where a man crawled behind a rock and moved toward him. He holstered his handgun to crawl better and snuck up behind the raider. The man, about five-ten, one sixty, spun around and saw Elmer's hulk coming at him and took the hard rush, face on, feeling ribs crack, and blood flow.

Elmer sat on the man's already broken chest and hit him three times with fists larger than melons. "He ain't dead, Puny and he ain't fightin' no more. How you doin with yours?"

"He's wounded, Elmer and hidden in that brush pile. Gonna light it off. That'll drive him out."

Elmer grabbed his man and jerked him to his feet, bringing squalls of pain from him and walked him to some rocks. "Sit still or die." He watched Puny light some twigs and get them ready to throw in the sun-dried brush, saw movement in the brush and motioned for Puny not to throw the torch. Elmer moved in and the man, holding a gun-shot arm, burst from the brush right into his arms.

Elmer simply picked the scrawny outlaw up, held him high in the air and threw him twenty feet or so to where Puny was standing. "He's all yours, Puny."

Puny put the torch out and picked the man up, whirled around once and flung him back at Elmer. "No, Elmer, you caught him fair and square. He's yours to do with as you please."

"Well, all right, then, we'll tie these two jaspers together and get the dead ones, too. One of us has to take them back to camp and the other has to stay and help Snake."

"I'll take 'em back, Elmer. You stay and help Snake. You need the exercise."

Getting the dead ones lashed to their horses took some time and then tying the wounded ones to their horses did too. "Almost dark, Puny. You gonna be good with this caravan? Be black dark by the time you reach the herd."

"I'll be fine. Do everything you can to get Fleming alive. A lot of people have been hurt by that man's shenanigans. All he cares about is money, doesn't have a decent bone in his body. I wish I'd thought to alert the sheriff to what I was doing."

"Almost out of his territory, I think," Elmer said. He watched Puny lead the four horses off on the trail back to camp, found his horse and rode toward the hillside where he thought Snake might be. "Hope that boy don't get anxious. Gotta take Fleming slow and with a lot of thinking." He could almost feel the darkness come on as he worked his way up the hillside, through palisades of rock, stands of cactus, trees and brush, toward where he thought Fleming might be.

***

"Not cut out to do your own dirty work, eh Major Fleming? I'm gonna teach you some manners old man." Snake murmured as he moved east a mile or two before he made his ascent, hoping to stumble onto Fleming's trail. "You ain't spent enough time away from that bank of yours, Major. Leaving a trail this open ain't the right way to guarantee a long life, sir."

Fleming didn't try to hide his trail at all, working

his way across the side of the hill and being able to see his four riders down in the valley. "Oh, my god," the horrified major said when he saw the puffs of rifle smoke and two of his men fall to the ground. He saw the entire production play out, right up to seeing the dead men tied to their horses.

"I've got to get back to Tucson," he murmured. "Gotta get a good alibi arranged. Sure as hell those fools that are alive will tell everything. Damn drunks." He moved up the side of the hill to where he had his horse tied off, just as fast as he could, not worrying about noise or being seen.

"Looking for something?" Snake stood next to Fleming's horse, pointing a rifle at the major. "Drop that rifle you've got and slowly undo your gun belt, Major. Time for a little face to face with April Theron. One of your men tried to kill Geneva and that lady is one angry mama bear right now. Do it, Major, before I forget I want you alive."

Fleming saw death in that rifle barrel, heard it in that voice and slowly let the rifle fall to the ground. But he made the mistake of his life when he went for his sidearm. Snake fired the rifle point blank, twice and Fleming's body was flung back eight feet or more.

"Damn fool, that's what you were. Or too much of a coward to face the hangman. Gonna be a long ride in the dark," he muttered. He had Fleming's body tied off and was working his way down the sidehill when Dog-man and Elmer rode up.

"I was hoping you'd need help," Dog-man said. "Shame you had to kill him, but I guess it's best in the long-run. Puny's gonna take the bodies and the prisoners back to Tucson in the morning. Near as I can tell, we haven't lost any time. I think we'll make Gila Bend just fine. What are we gonna do about April and that ranch?"

"Just as we talked, Partner. Ain't no changes. This fool might be dead, but she still owes on that mortgage and she still needs a foreman."

"You applying for that job, Snake? You'd end up with a wife and kids if you are." There weren't any chuckles, no sneers, just the truth as Dog-man saw it. "Man could do a whole lot worse than April. Yes, sir, a whole lot worse."

Snake ignored the comments and rode slowly down the hillside, wondering just where all of this might lead. They had ridden for almost an hour before Snake said, "I ain't looking to be foreman or having a family."

And just why ain't I? That thought worried him all the way back to camp and he couldn't shake it. *I got enough money to make that ranch right, she's mighty good lookin', and I love those kids all to pieces. It ain't me, that's why. It just ain't me.*

15

"That's the whole story, Sheriff." Puny Russell was sitting in a chair across from Sheriff Ansel Williams after delivering the bodies and prisoners. "Fleming was doing everything he could to keep Mrs. Theron from getting that herd to Gila Bend."

"He's had this coming for some time, Puny, but it would have been best if it was the law what done him in. How far out were they? My jurisdiction ends out that way some."

"Hadn't crossed the county line, Ansel. Me and Elmer Spaulding are in full agreement with that. At least half a mile inside the county. You plannin' on riding out to talk with Mrs. Theron?"

"Naw, not with your testimony. No reason to." Sheriff Williams cocked his head to one side, as if thinking about something. "Might want to talk to that Snake person when they get back. Heard a report about him gettin' into it with Crabby Pete Keaton."

Puny chuckled. "Everybody gets into it with Keaton, but I don't think Snake and Dog-man were planning on coming back once the herd is sold."

"Maybe I will take a ride out to Gila Bend. Ain't been in that country for some time. Help me get these wounded ones over to Doc McCarthy's." Sheriff Williams hollered into the back of the jail for a deputy to get the bodies delivered to the undertaker.

"How many pieces of property are going to be affected by Fleming's death?" Puny knew just about every farmer and rancher in the valley and figured that many were still paying off their mortgages. "Fleming also controls the bank and other businesses right in town. There'll be some changes around old Tucson, I'm a-thinkin'."

Many eyes saw Puny lead his caravan through town and word of Fleming's death spread like wildfire. Major Fleming carried paper on half a dozen or more businesses in the ancient citadel and even more ranches in the valley. How would his death affect those people? Who would be collecting payments? Questions were being asked in every quarter of the city.

After delivering the wounded to McCarthy, the sheriff headed back to his office and Puny Russell went to his own business where he found a number of people waiting to talk to him. They gathered around a large table in the back of the store, five in chairs, the rest standing. "Looks like we got a lot of questions," Puny said, "and not very many answers. Territorial judge will have to do the answering boys. Fleming's accounts will have to be handled lawfully even if the man himself often didn't have much to do with the law end of his dealings."

"Wish I'd been there to help shoot him," one old timer said. "I still owe five hundred on my place and don't know how I'm gonna pay it off." The group grumbled for several more minutes before breaking up and nobody left knowing any more than when they arrived.

***

Ansel Williams was packing his saddlebags with some trail food when the deputy returned from delivering the bodies. "Heading over to Gila Bend. Be gone several days, Bo, so keep the lid on things around here."

Williams was tall and thin, rangy, with long legs, long arms and a long face that seldom smiled. Even his massive mustache drooped and hung down some. He was Missouri born, spent his early years in the Territories, slipped south into Texas, always carrying a badge. He was slow to use his guns feeling comfortable with fists and feet or talking a man down.

"If you find a couple of hours, Bo, head out to the Theron place and make sure everything's all right. Indians haven't been raising any hell since their attack, but it is the last place out and there are some cattle left."

Beauregard Carradine nodded and slumped down in the sheriff's chair. Williams had to laugh as he walked out to start his ride to Gila Bend, about sixty miles on the road. He had his bedroll, slicker, and plenty of food for the ride. "Crabby Pete said Snake just up and shot him, but the Dawson men said that wasn't so. I'd sure believe the Dawson men over Crabby Pete." Williams muttered with himself often on long rides like this.

"Doctor McCarthy said the Theron ranch would

have been burnt to the ground if it weren't for Snake and Dog-man, Puny Russell said the two have done nothing but help since they arrived. Maybe I'm riding out just coz I want to ride out for a day or two." There was no smile, but a hint of a chuckle as he nudged his horse into a nice, miles eating trot.

***

"How much further, Elmer? I'm thinkin' we'll be in Gila Bend sometime tomorrow, but you know this country, I don't." Snake was standing near the morning fire, tin-cup of coffee in hand. "Been a good drive despite our troubles. Didn't lose five head. Didn't have to push 'em too hard, either."

"We'll be there tomorrow, Snake." The big man settled down on his haunches and poured more coffee. "I'm gonna ride in today and make arrangements for the herd. April gave me her letter of authorization for the sale. She wanted to ride in with me, but she needs to stay with the herd."

"That's best," Snake said. "Make sure she and the kids have a place to stay. It's gonna take fifty gallons of hot water to get the trail dust off Hank. He's rode drag almost from the start." It was laughter from the two, not chuckles that Dog-man heard walking up to the fire.

"Mornin'. What's so funny?"

"Talkin' about Hank and that cloud of dust he owns." Snake said. "I think he just picked up his nick-name, Dog. We'll call him Dusty from now on. Dusty Theron. Elmer thinks we'll make Gila Bend tomorrow."

"We made good time once we got Fleming out

of the picture. You talked with April this morning?" Dog-man poured some coffee. "I hope she's prepared for what that sale is going to bring. That's not a good-looking bunch of sale cattle out there."

"I think she knows that, but she's a strong lady, Dog. She knows she has a big decision to make when she hires a foreman. Geneva's gonna drive the wagon and April's gonna ride alongside me this morning to talk about that."

"Don't be forever with that talk. It'll just be me and Hank with the herd. We'll need you and Geneva as soon as possible."

"You're right. Elmer's riding into town. Maybe I'll drive the wagon and let you have Geneva right away."

Snake found April and Geneva harnessing the team and sent Geneva to join Dog-man and Hank. "We got a lot to talk about, April."

"I've thought about your thoughts on hiring a good foreman, Snake. I have one in mind." She smiled at him as she got a hand up to the seat. "I'd be pleased if you would take the job." She reached over and put her hand on Snake's arm. "I know the children would love it."

There it is, he thought, the one question he didn't want to have to answer. Snake did not have friendly thoughts about relationships with women. Truth be told, he was afraid of most women and their smiles, warmth, and wiles.

Dog-man is always saying how wonderful it would be to have a relationship, a wife, a family. If it's so wonderful, why doesn't he have one? This is a lovely, charming lady, I do enjoy her children, but how long would it be before I'd feel trapped? Want to move on? No, it would not be fair to her, me, or those kids.

"I'm a drifter, April," Snake said. He wanted to give her a big smile but couldn't. He wanted to tell her flat out, no and would also like to tell her yes, knowing down the line the ranch, her, and the kids would be his. That's what scared him most. Her and the kids, not having the ranch. *I could run the ranch, sure as all get out, but bein' a husband? A father? My Lordy and all the sand in Texas.*

"I'm not a settlin' down kind of man. Never been in one place long enough to have a suit of clothes hangin'. Ain't much good at this kind of talk, either." He had the wagon moving along toward the herd and kept his eyes on the leaders. He kept hearing little tinkles of laughter from her, didn't dare look her in the eye.

"You need a man who will do you and the children right, not a drifter thinkin' about where the next trail might lead. Me and Dog are heading for California and we don't even know why."

She had to chuckle at the way he was trying to say no to her wonderful offer. "The job and everything that goes with it is yours, Snake, if you change your mind." She let her mind drift, wondering what it would be like living with a man who could think, put his thoughts into words and act on those words. "Promise me you'll help me find a good foreman?"

"I promise, April. I do for sure, promise." It was a quiet ride for the next hour, with Snake and April working their way through their thoughts. "You'll be a fine husband and father someday, Snake. I wish I'd met someone like you before I met Rufus."

"It's a long trail I've been on, April and there's thousands of miles left to travel. You have your ranch and I have an open trail. I couldn't live your way and I know you couldn't live mine. I'll not leave you until I have a fine foreman for your ranch." *Am I thinking straight? I'm throwing away a magnificent woman, three beautiful children, and what could be a thriving ranch. For what? Why?*

For Snake, those questions simply couldn't be answered. Why did he and Dog-man simply ride away from their producing mine? Why did they walk away from good jobs with George Dawson and his freight business? For that matter, why did they leave that ranch near Denver? Neither Dog-man nor Snake could tell you, but the lure of the open road was far stronger than the concept of being settled, having a comfortable and safe life.

16

"So that's what Gila Bend looks like," Dog-man said, leading the herd over a ridge. "That's a fair-sized river." He had Geneva riding the left side of the herd and Snake on the right, with Dusty thriving at drag. "Hope Elmer comes up to lead us to the sale yards. Can't tell from up here where we're going."

He could see how the village got its name, the river taking a great turn. He got his answer about a guide in less than half an hour when two drovers rode up to the herd. "This the Theron herd?"

"Is indeed," Dog-man said. "You pointing the way for us?"

"Am, indeed," the drover said, almost mocking Dog-man. "Names Daniels, George Daniels," he said, offering both a smile and his hand. "This here's Sean O'Grady."

"Glad to meet you, boys. They call me Dog-man and that's Snake over yonder. Mrs. Theron's driving the wagon. Ain't seen a river like that in a long time."

"You can follow it down to an even bigger one," Daniels said. "Steamboats, boats with sails, come all the way up from the Cortez Sea."

"You're foolin' with me," Dog-man said. "Steam-boats in this desert?"

"It's the truth," O'Grady laughed. "Seen 'em myself."

Dog-man sat still, mesmerized, looking out across the rugged Arizona Territory desert, trying to imagine a river flowing through that would be big enough to accommodate a steamboat. *Wouldn't that be something to see? I gotta tell Snake about this. We gotta see this.*

George Daniels dropped back and rode up to the wagon. "Morning, Mrs. Theron," he said. "Name's George Daniels. Gonna lead your herd right up to the sale pens. Sales will begin tomorrow, so your herd will be settled."

"Glad to meet you, Mr. Daniels. Afraid it's not the best herd you've ever seen. I've had some problems."

"I've heard. Mr. Spaulding's been a friend for some time. I'm sorry for your loss, Ma'am. Chatterbox Andy will work hard and get you the best prices possible."

"Chatterbox? I'm afraid I don't understand," April said.

Daniels had to laugh. "He's the auctioneer, Mrs. Theron. He can talk a million words a minute, I think. Chatterbox Andy will be selling your herd." April smiled and nodded, and George had to smile when he realized she had probably never been to a livestock sale, never heard an auctioneer.

He rode alongside the wagon, talked about cattle, prices and the markets and April enjoyed the company. George was a big man, stout, with a fast and friendly smile, bright eyes, and sat a horse like he was born to it. It isn't often, she thought, that inside of less than a month she had met three men with goods manners and who treated her children properly.

"Tell me about the sale, Mr. Daniels. I've not been here before. Have you worked there for some time?"

"No," he said. "Came down from Utah a couple of years ago, but the job I was coming to wasn't there. The old man that owned the ranch died and it was sold. Went to work for Kirby Sunderland at the stockyard. He's a fair man to work for, but it ain't my kind of work."

"Your kind of work is cattle, though, right?"

"That it is. Spent some time in Texas, moved north to Nebraska country for a while, but this is the kind of country I really love. Big, open, tough. Well, about the stockyards," George said, "they're clean, cattle are well cared for before and during the sales and the people are easy to get along with."

"That's good to hear. We've been on the drive for two weeks now. I hope Mr. Spaulding has found me a hotel with a bath. I must be a mess." April chuckled, thinking about how much dust and dirt she must be carrying.

"Oh, no Ma'am, you're just fine," George said, then blushed and tried to say something else, bringing more giggles from April. "Maybe I'd best get up with the herd," he said. "Talk to you later."

"I hope so." April said, almost under her breath. *My, God. What on earth am I doing? Rufe just died and I'm being all girlish with this man. I'm a better person than that, but after meeting Snake and Dog-man, I've changed. Have I really? No, it's the lonely, that's what it is. Being with Rufe was the same as being alone. Just simple conversation was beyond that man. Talking with Snake and Dog-man has come so easy. It's like I've awakened from a long cold night.*

***

Sean O'Grady was talking with Snake when Daniels rode back up to the front of the drive. "This here's Snake," he said. "He and Dog-man have brought the herd in for Mrs. Theron. Snake, meet George Daniels."

"Howdy," Snake said. He reached out to take the man's hand. "Been a good drive in, but the herd wasn't much to talk about when we started. Mrs. Theron's had some bad times, I'm afraid. Elmer get us all set up?"

"Got all the paperwork done and pens are ready for you. What part of Texas you hail from? Bexar's my country."

"Anywhere and everywhere," Snake laughed. "Mostly along the Colorado. I like this country, though."

It took another several hours to move the herd into the stockyards and get them penned. Food and water were plentiful, the yardmen had everything under controlm and Dog-Man and Snake settled in at a table in the nearest saloon. "Beer, my man," Snake said after catching the barman's eye. "Cold and keep 'em coming."

The barman had welcomed hundreds of drovers over the years, knew his beer was cold, and gave the boys a warm smile. He was skinny, had a shiny head with just wisps of hair, here and there and smiling eyes. "You the boys just bring that scrawny herd in? Hope you got some money now cuz you won't have much after the sale."

"Bad times for that family," Snake said. "Bad times." The saloon was a long, narrow affair with the bar and a couple of tables up front and more tables and gambling in the rear. He clinked mugs with Dog-man and drained the glass. "Oh, my, yes," he said. "Many more like this and I'll live."

"What are we gonna do, Snake? We got April here, and she ain't gonna have enough to pay off that mortgage. Are you sure we should jump into that mess?"

"It is a mess, Dog, that's for sure. I promised April that I would find her a good cowman to be her foreman and we've already agreed to help her out. She owes five hundred dollars and she ain't gonna see half that from this sale." Snake's eyes had narrowed, and his chin jutted out some, thinking about April and the children.

"You're thinking about Geneva and Hank, I mean, Dusty, aren't you?" Dog-man had a slight smile on his face. "And little Terry. Why don't you just marry the woman, Snake?"

"Couldn't do that, Dog. Bustin' up our partnership? Yes, I'd miss you, dreadful, but sittin' at the same table every night forever? I'd enjoy being with April, I'd just love all over those kids, but sooner than later, I'd miss the open road, Dog, and it would kill me to ride off, but I'd do it. Sure as all hell, I'd do it."

It was a quiet table for the next round of cold beer, Dog-man thinking about steamboats in the desert and Snake thinking about how lovely April was and how much he felt for the children. "Best get to the hotel and make sure April's settled in proper," Snake said.

"Sean Grady told me that if we follow this river on downstream we'll come to an even bigger river with steamboats cruising about. I think he's feedin' me some stuff, Snake. You ever heard of such a thing?"

"Ben Rhyerson told me all about them boats, Dog. Got big ferries to get you across the river, too. Get on the other side and you're in California. Did you know that?"

"You know all that and you ain't said nothing? You ever been on a steamboat?"

"Ain't never ever even seen one, Dog. Heard tell they blow up from time to time."

***

Supper in the hotel dining room was controlled chaos. They shoved several tables together despite the unwillingness of the staff. April, her drovers, as she called Snake, Dog-man, and Elmer, the children, and George Daniels made up the party of eight. "This has been the most exciting experience of my life," April said. Her smile was more than generous. "I'm actually sorry the drive had to end."

"Why can't we buy more cows to go home with?" Hank said. "You and me could do that, Snake."

"Probably could, little man, as long as you ride drag."

April saw it in Hank's eyes, knew exactly how Geneva and Terry felt, and had to admit, she too, wanted Snake to be their father. *Why couldn't I have met a man like that? Why?* She could feel the tears coming on and wasn't going to let that happen. "Isn't that something you said, earlier, George? That we should pick up a few prime heifers at the sale to enhance our herd?"

George Daniels cleared his throat and took a quick glance toward Snake. "You said you left some good heifers at the ranch, you have some good bulls, it wouldn't hurt. You'd need a crew, though."

"We got a crew," Geneva said. "Me and Dusty, Snake and Dog-man, and mama and Elmer." She smiled at Snake. "Best crew in the territory."

"It would be, but me and Snake won't be riding back with you."

The silence at the table was broken by the quiet sniffles that Hank tried to hold back.

17

"You gotta come back with us," Geneva said. She and Snake were standing at the bottom of the staircase that led up to the hotel rooms. "Mama needs you, Snake. I need you. You saved us from the Indians, you brought our herd here. Me and Hank and Terry need a father."

"Oh, you little darlin'," Snake said, so quiet she wasn't sure she really heard him. "You ain't quite old enough to know the different kinds of people there are in this old world of ours. My kind just ain't fit for staying in one place for a long time. My kind just rides off after a time, and people get hurt because of it."

He could see the hurt in her eyes, saw the lower lip quiver, felt anger at himself. "See what I mean? I haven't even rode off and I've hurt you. I love you and Hank and Terry very much, but, girl, I know me. I know I would ride off someday. I'm gonna find a good man to be your mama's foreman and your mama will find a good man to be her husband and your papa."

He watched the tears roll down Geneva's face as the girl turned and fled up the stairs. *Please don't hate me, girl, but it's just the way I am. Dog better be in that saloon and I ain't drinkin' beer tonight.*

Snake slipped through the doors and into the hotel saloon, saw Dog-man sitting with Elmer Spaulding and George Daniels and pulled up a chair. "You look like death warmed over," Dog-man said.

"It'll be worse tomorrow," Snake said. He poured whiskey in his glass and stared at it for a moment before taking a sip. "I just hurt Geneva something horrible." He was about to go on when a tall thin man wearing a shiny badge came up to the table.

"You the one called Snake?"

"I am. What can I do for you, Sheriff?" He started to get up, but the sheriff shook him off.

"Name's Williams, from Tucson. Puny told me how you and Mrs. Theron were able to put an end to Major Fleming's plans. Howdy, Elmer. She and the children doing well?"

"They're upstairs in their rooms, Sheriff. The sale is tomorrow. I'm afraid it won't be one of her best days. I doubt you rode all the way out here to ask about that wonderful family, eh?" Elmer gave Snake a knowing smile.

Sheriff Williams chuckled and sat down. "No, I didn't. You the one called Dog-man?" He looked at Dog-man and got a nod. "Good." He turned back to Snake. "Understand you shot Crabby Pete Keaton. Have a reason for doing that?"

"Oh, I did, Sheriff. Nasty man, Keaton. He was fixin' to shoot me and I don't like bein' shot. Ben Rhyerson will back me. Those two miners will too."

"They have, I just wanted to hear you come right

out and say you shot the man. Keaton left out the part of him wanting to shoot you. I'll see you at the sale tomorrow." Williams got up, nodded to the table and walked toward the hotel entrance.

"Now there's a different kind of sheriff, Dog. Never once tried to call me an outlaw. I like him." Snake turned to George and gave him a long look, took a drink of whiskey, and lit a cigar. "April said you ain't too happy working the sale pens, George. What about working the open range, tending a run-down, but with good water and grass, ranch? You up to something like that?"

"Been looking for something like that." George smiled, lit his own cigar, and poured drinks around. He wanted to say more, wanted to say he would almost grovel to get the job of foremen at the Theron place. "You have something in mind, Snake?"

"Mrs. Theron's ranch is pitiful in many respects, George, but there is good water and plentiful grass. She's got a rough row to hoe, ain't got hired help, ain't got a man anymore, and has three kids that have grown up in the last couple of weeks. I promised her I would find a good cowman to be her foreman and I think you would fill that bill just fine. Guaranteed there wouldn't be much pay, there would be plenty of hard work, and it could be a fine ranch."

Snake wanted to say there were other possibilities but didn't. That would be up to April, and more likely, the children. "You'd be pestered often by rambunctious children asking a million questions, but you'd be well fed."

"I thought you were the foreman," George said. "I had a lot of envy because of that. There isn't anything I'd rather be than foreman of that spread. I ain't that good at talkin', Snake. What do I do, just walk up and ask for the job? Those kids are rascals and love their ranch. She's most attractive and would fight hard to keep it. I've always wanted to ramrod an outfit that needed help."

Dog-man caught the eye of one of the ladies serving drinks and motioned for another round. When she brought a tray full of beer mugs and a bottle of whiskey, a man jumped up and smacked her hard enough to knock her to the ground. "Spill your beer on someone else, woman," he snarled. He raised his foot to kick her in the head but found himself face down on the filthy floor. George Daniels had him pinned.

The heavy Daniels slammed the man's head onto the floor three times, jumped to his feet and helped get the cocktail lady up. "How bad hurt are you? Here, sit down and catch your breath."

George was busy and didn't notice the instigator's friends coming toward him. One had a big skinning knife at the ready. Snake and Dog-man saw them, though and met the charge with one of their own. Snake took on the man with the knife by putting two rounds from his revolver through his heart, which in turn stopped everything in the saloon. George slowly stood straight up and walked to the man who knocked the woman down.

He jerked him to his feet and drove his fist into the man's groin, twice. "Real men don't hit women, mister," and he hit him again, but this time right between the eyes. He let the man slowly sink back to the floor, helped the cocktail waitress up from the chair, and handed her tray back.

"Thank you," she murmured. She was crying,

wiping blood from her nose, trying to ease her way through the mass of men gathered around. Two of the other cocktail women came to her rescue and eased her out of the crowd.

"All right, break it up." The deputy city marshal shoved people aside trying to get to the scene. "Who did what and why?" He was a burly man, overly large hands, long arms, and a barrel chest. "Well? Man didn't shoot himself, did he?"

"I shot him," Snake said. "Came at me with that knife. Had to."

The deputy marshal looked around. "That the way it happened?" Most of the men nodded, some turned away, nobody said no. "All right then. What about this yahoo. Why is he wallowing around on the floor? Well?"

"I busted him a couple of times for beating on one of the saloon girls," George said.

The deputy marshal looked around, got many nods and no shakes of the head. "Well, then, let's get the body out of here. Everything that happened was justified as far as I'm concerned." He pointed at a couple of men to help him carry the body out and left.

Dog-man stood next to Snake. "Second time in a row, Dog. I'm starting to like Arizona Territory. Lawmen in New Mexico all wanted to call us outlaws. These here law dogs actually listen to what we say." He was shaking his head, took a beer from an offered tray and continued.

"George didn't hesitate knocking that thug down." Dog-man smiled and took a long drink of cold beer. "I think April's gonna be just fine. You wasted a bullet, though. Only needed to shoot the knife man once."

"I'll be more careful in the future, Dog." The three men sat back down and over an hour or two, finished off the bottle. "Join us for breakfast, George and be prepared to tell Mr. Sunderland at the stockyards you might be leaving," Snake said. "George, Elmer, Dog, I'm calling it a night."

Snake should be smiling, after all he just fulfilled his promise to April, but he was also losing an opportunity for a life of hard work and happiness, a life with a warm and lovely woman, and a built in family. He grabbed a fresh bottle and headed for the stockyards. He was sleeping with the wagon and all the horses. *I don't want to think about nothing. Nothing.*

***

Bidding on the Theron lots was slow and low and there was little enthusiasm among the buyers. Snake and April were standing off to the side of the show ring watching. April showed her strength by not crying at the pitiful prices and took the tin cup full of coffee that Snake offered.

Earlier that morning, Snake and Dog-man sat with her at the seller's table, having fresh sweet rolls and coffee. "Guess you and your crew will be heading back tomorrow, eh?" Snake was looking her right in the eye.

"I'll always have a spot for you, Snake. Thank you for George Daniels. You're a man of your word. We'll drive what few heifers we can acquire back with us. I don't know how I'll pay that mortgage, but I'll figure something out."

"We want to talk to you about that," Dog-man said. Snake pulled an envelope from his coat and handed it to her.

"What's this?" Her hands were shaking as she opened it and she gasped at what she found. "No," she almost whimpered. "Oh, my God." There were five one hundred-dollar bills inside and a note. She took the note out and read it, the boys sat quiet, watching tears flow in a torrent. She pressed the note and the envelope tightly to her breast and looked back and forth at Dog-man and Snake.

"I can't take this," she said. "You can't do this."

"Well, April, you must take it. Me and old Dog here ain't your run-of-the-mill drifters, and we like to see good people come out of top. Might come through this way again one day and we'd want a good supper and warm bed of straw in the barn. Don't let Geneva keep trying to talk like me and George. Ain't fit for a lady."

***

"How long before they're married?" Dog-man and Snake were standing at the fence watching April and her crew ride out. Geneva, George, and Elmer were driving fifteen fine heifers and Dusty was riding drag, a mile-wide smile on his young face. April had the wagon lined out and waved back at them.

"She's a proper lady, Dog, but they'll be married within six months, guaranteed. George is a good man and he'll be a fine father to those kids." Snake turned away, afraid of what Dog-man might see. He wiped an arm across his face, as if to wipe away sweat and walked toward their horses. "Have any idea where we're goin? Or why?"

"Best if we follow the sun, Snake. Little town called Yuma out that way and that's where we'll find steamboats and a big river. I was talking with Sean O'Grady during the sale. Just follow that road west and we'll be there, he said."

"Best get it on, then. Don't want to miss the steamboats," Snake drawled out. "Sure gonna miss those kids, though."

18

It was the morning of the second day on the trail. "Ain't seen that much dust in a long time," Snake said. A big cloud was boiling up half a mile in front of them. "Dust, Dog, or smoke?" They were just hours from Yuma, passed a couple of ranches and had been talking about steamboats.

Waves of heat blurred the vision, with nary a breeze to be had. They had been on the trail just a few hours and were hoping to find a copse of trees that might offer a piece of shade. "I'm not sure, Dog, but I am sure I can see some trees near that dust."

"That's smoke for sure," Dog-man said. "That's a ranch, Snake and something big is on fire." They put the horses and the pack mule they bought from Kirby Sunderland into a nice trot. "That's a barn, Snake. A big barn and it's a gonner."

They turned into the lane leading to a ranch house standing off from the burning barn. Four people were carrying buckets back and forth from the house well. "Better give 'em a hand, Dog, even though it's a losing cause." They tied off and ran to help only to find a big shotgun aimed right at them.

"One more step and you both die," the woman said. She was joined by a man holding a rifle, and two children, one with a pitch-fork, the other with an ax. "You working for Chastain? Here to gloat are you?" The woman was about thirty, skinny and with long blondish hair wrapped in a bun.

"No, Ma'am," Snake said. "Saw the smoke, came to help. Don't know nobody named Chastain." He kept his hands well away from his sidearm, saw Dog-man do the same, and tried to smile. The array of weapons was fearful. "I'm Snake and this here's Dog-man, We was riding in from Gila Bend. Looks like that barn's a total loss, I'm afraid."

Maybe it was the Texas in his voice, maybe it was the kindness in his eyes, but Snake eased the woman's mind enough that she lowered the shotgun. "If I find out you're Chastain's men I'll pull both triggers," she said.

"I don't think they are, Ginny. Don't look mean enough." The man took a step forward and stuck out his hand. "Name's Otter. Jeremiah Otter. This here's my missus, Virginia and our kids, Jake and Becky. Thank you for riding in even if it was too late to help any."

The heat from the inferno drove the group back some and when a wall caved in on itself, they had to move back even further. Hot cinders rose high into the air and black clouds of dense smoke could probably be seen from miles around. "I can rebuild the barn," Jeremiah said. "Sure glad I got the animals out. That would have been the end for us."

"Who's this Chastain feller? Why would someone want to burn your barn?" Dog-man was more curious than good manners would dictate but Ginny Otter let him know the answers right away.

"Man's an out and out criminal, that's who he is. Has the Bordertown Saloon and Dancehall in Yuma and runs gambling on the steamboats. We owe him money from a crooked deal he offered some of the ranchers in the valley."

"One at a time, he's been burning people out. The one's that owe him," Jeremiah said. "I guess we were next on the list, but his men got seen before they put the torch to the house and Ginny run 'em off with that shotgun of hers." He was able to get a slight grin on his face.

"Cowards," little Jake said. "I hollered, but they was on fast horses."

"Said you just come in from Gila Bend, eh? What's bringing you to Yuma? Lots of sand and a muddy river." Jeremiah Otter said.

Snake looked at Dog-man, then back to Otter. "Sounds silly, I guess. We ain't never seen a steamboat." At the end of his comment he was looking at the tip ends of his boots and when eight-year-old Becky, still holding that mean looking ax, started laughing, Snake wanted to mount up and ride off. "Well, we ain't."

Virginia was trying to hold back her giggles. "They're big, some are beautiful, but they're rat infested. Most of those rats are grifters, gamblers, card sharks, every low thing a man can do is done on those boats and Millard Chastain runs the lot of 'em."

Snake saw a lot of hatred in the woman's face, along with a generous dose of determination. *Seen three kinds of woman on this little journey of ours,* he thought. He liked the way the lady held her head, the way her chin jutted out some. *Mercy Potter was helpless and played on it, April Theron was fast learning what this Ginny lady already knows. This world ain't for the faint of heart. Gotta fight and protect every inch of the way.*

"What good are these big boats in a river in the middle of the desert?" Dog-man was shaking his head. "Does that river go somewhere?" More giggles from the children and Dog-man had to duck his head some.

"They tell me it runs straight out of the Rocky Mountains," Otter said. "But what's important, it empties into the Sea of Cortez just a few miles south. Ocean going vessels unload goods for Phoenix and other points north and they're loaded on the steamboats and brought here. Big business, lots of money involved."

"That's where outlaws like Chastain come into the picture," Virginia said. "Boats carry passengers, passengers like to gamble, Chastain doesn't run fair games." The hatred was molasses thick as she spelled out the problems.

"By golly," Snake whispered. Dog-man looked at him and could almost visualize a ride south and then back north on a steamboat. "We'll be heading into Yuma," Snake said. "Anybody we should look up and tell about the fire? Anything we can send back?"

"Might let the sheriff know, but ain't nothin' he'll do. Chastain tells him what to do." Virginia said. "If you run into a man named Johnny Simon, he's a carriage maker and wheelwright, he would want to know. A shirt-tail relative of sorts. Good man." Jeremiah nodded his head, slipped an arm around his wife and pulled her close.

***

"She's an angry woman, Dog. Wouldn't want her mad at me. We sure ain't tellin' the sheriff nothin', either, if he's an outlaw. We've met those kind. Let's make up camp before we get to town and ride in fresh in the morning. That woman gave us some fresh meat and eggs for the morning."

"Must be some kind of big river," Dog-man said. "I've seen the Missouri and it's impressive. Like to see New Orleans sometime, maybe. Out on the prairie, in them little towns, there's always a gambler or two, but in them river towns, it seems, the gamblers all get together." He had to laugh. "Heard one man say it seemed like they all nested up along the rivers."

Snake saw the river before he saw Yuma and pulled his horse to a stop. "My goodness and all gracious, too," he said. "Ain't that a sight. Right in the middle of the desert."

They rode into a small grassy spot several hundred yards off the road and made up camp. "Can't get that fire out of my mind," Dog-man said. "To hire somebody to burn out a family! That's as low as a man can get. Hope we don't run into this Chastain. Might just shoot him."

"Might be a good reason to run into him," Snake chuckled. "Man needs shooting."

They talked about steamboats, crooked gamblers, and barn fires well into dark and crawled into the bedrolls. "Just look at them stars, Dog. Looks like I can reach out and grab one or run my hand around and get 'em all scrambled up. Some men like their buildings and soft beds and some like the feel of the ground and the looks of the sky. Open desert or high mountains, if I can see the sky I'm happy."

"You gonna be all right giving up April Theron? You'd a made a fine father for them kids."

"It would have been wonderful, but only for a short time. I'da got to thinking about nights like this and run off, Dog. You know I woulda. I did the right thing." It wasn't easy to say and Snake wasn't sure he was even telling the truth. *The truth? What is the truth? I might very well live to regret what I've done.* Was Snake afraid of the truth? How many times had he told Dog-man that women frightened him? Maybe Snake was afraid of April simply because he had never had a serious relationship with a woman. Maybe it wasn't these thoughts of longing for the open trail.

"That's enough talk about April, steamboats, and burning barns for tonight, Dog."

Sleep came fast for the two, but a couple of hours later, Dog-Man sat straight up, hearing horses coming toward their camp. "Visitors, Snake. Coming hard."

Snake found some bushes to his left and Dog-man crawled into a small wash to the right. Both men had their sidearms and rifles and were ready when three men rode right up to the camp.

"Burn everything you see and kill the two saddle bums. They tried to help Otter and that mouthy wife of his," one of the men said. Snake's rifle spat fire and the man fell dead beside his horse. The other two dropped to the ground pulling their weapons. Dog-man fired once, putting a bullet through one of the men's legs.

The wounded man was hurt bad and was crying out for help, but his partner was too busy trying to find cover. He thought he saw someone and fired his revolver twice into a tree, giving his position away. Snake's second shot put him down for good.

"You, with the busted-up leg, throw that gun out where I can see it," Dog-man yelled. "Do it or I kill you where you lie." He watched the man throw his sidearm into the dirt. "You got a rifle or shotgun with you? Answer me."

"Ain't got one. Oh, this hurts. Help me," the man cried out.

Snake and Dog-man moved slowly toward the wounded man, found him unarmed and bleeding badly. The rifle slug had not only ripped through an artery, it shattered the thigh bone bad enough for it to come right through the skin.

"So, you're the bastards that tried to burn out the Otter family, eh?" Snake dragged the screaming man toward where the fire had been and got it restarted. "Otter said you work for Millard Chastain. That right?"

"Who are you to ask?"

"I'm the man's gonna let you die if you don't answer," Snake said.

The outlaw was silent for a moment and then said, "yeah, we work for Chastain. You gonna get me help? Damn, it hurts." The blood was flowing from the ripped artery and the man's eyes rolled back into his head. He was too weak to talk and Snake let the life flow out of him.

"Ain't nothing I could have done, Dog. His leg bone was shattered, and blood was flowing like a waterfall. The other two dead?"

"No doubt," Dog-man said. "They must have followed us when we left Otter's place. Clean their pockets and get 'em buried. Don't plan on talking about this when we get to Yuma."

"Ain't nobody's business but ours," Snake said. "See? If we was in a building and in a soft bed, ain't none of this woulda happened."

"Yup. Woulda been a dumb way for us to die, though, shot up by some bad men who don't even know our names."

It was getting light by the time they had the outlaws in the ground. "Grizzly business, Dog. How do you want your eggs? Some good side meat, too. Virginia Otter might be a mean woman to men she don't like, but she sure took care of us."

19

"River's even bigger when you're right up to it," Dog-man said. It was late morning, hot and windy, when the boys rode into Yuma. "Old town, Snake. Been here since them conquistadores, I do believe."

"I don' think I've ever been this hot or uncomfortable," Snake said. He was lounged back taking in all the sights and sounds. "Cervesa, Dog, look for a building with that word plastered large. Cold cervesa, by the barrel."

They were riding into the central plaza of the old Spanish town. Like most, it was laid out as a wheel with streets coming out of the plaza as spokes. Central to the plaza was the church, which was surrounded by businesses of every sort and kind. Wagons, carts, people leading laden donkeys and burros, and mounted riders threaded their way. No one seemed to be in any particular hurry.

"That's a fine-looking cantina over that way." Snake pointed off to their right as they entered the center of the village. "Could use some meat and chilies, Dog."

"Maybe a barrel or two of cold beer, too? Interesting country. Ain't like the country we've been in. Can you ranch it?" Dog-man asked. "We been riding in some sparse feed. In Missouri, they say, one acre will feed a cow. Here it might take ten acres or more."

Dog turned his horse toward the cantina and Snake followed, leading their mule. "Let's get the animals settled," Snake said. "Then find some good food and check out the riverfront. Looks like corrals and blacksmith shop at the end of the street."

"More than that, Snake. The sign says Simon Wagon Works. Must be Johnny Simon's place. Might be a good time to make a friend from a shirt-tail relative." They tied off at a hitch rack in front of the wagon works and slipped into the generous building.

"Would you look at that," Snake said. He nodded at a well-appointed and almost finished carriage. He walked over and let his hands rub over the fine finish. "My goodness, someone will be riding in high style."

"Help you gents?" An old man sucking on a cold pipe stepped out from the office. His hands were gnarled from years of working with wood tools, his shoulders were slouched some, but his eyes were bright. If one were to look close, Snake thought, one would see a lifetime of good humor.

"You Johnny Simon?" Snake asked.

"Nope. Johnny's over to the cantina. Sumpin' I can help you with?" The old man had a friendly look on his face, not the least worried about two strangers coming in.

"Nope. Never met the man but got a message for

him from Virginia Otter. What's he look like? We'll have some dinner and cold beer, too."

"Johnny's about as tall as you and with another fifty pounds for good measure. Wearing a red shirt and black vest. He's got a full, very red beard and wears his hair long. About the best man I've ever worked for." The old man nodded, worked to fill his pipe, and sauntered back to the office.

"I bet that old man's just as tough as he is friendly," Snake said. "I can already taste a bowl of chili and a dozen tortillas, Dog. Break open a new keg of beer and let's hear the music." He did a little two-step, kicked some dust, and started for the cantina. "We can leave the animals right here, Dog."

***

"You ain't gonna flim-flam me like you do others, Chastain. You want that carriage finished you get it paid for. That was our deal. You have it paid for before picking it up. You're one hundred dollars shy of that and I'm less than ten hours from having that little gem ready for a team of high prancing coursers."

Millard Chastain had busted his way into a conversation Simon was having with Pedro Gonzalez, owner of Pedro's Cantina. Chastain was demanding that a carriage he had on order be ready for him to pick up that afternoon. "You have that carriage ready for me tomorrow at noon, Simon and you'll have your hundred dollars. I'll spread the word from Phoenix to Mexico, I'll tell the world what a bad wagon maker you are. I'll have you begging for business."

"I'll not only not beg for your business, I refuse to ever do business with you again. Best to stay out of my path, Chastain. The world knows a four-flusher when it sees one."

"You bastard." Chastain growled and had his bowie knife out, threatening Johnny Simon. "I'm going to slice you top to bottom, wagon maker."

"Ain't gonna do no such thing, gambling man." Snake waved Johnny Simon back a step, aimed the big Colt at Chastain's chest, and motioned for him to drop the knife. Chastain was taken by complete surprise. No one in Yuma talked to him that way. No one drew a gun on Millard Chastain and lived to tell about it.

The gambler was a slight man, dressed in silk blouse covered by a satin vest. Arrogance spread across his face as he looked around to see who might be watching and found Dog-man very close and holding a sidearm as well. Quick, faster than Snake or Dog-man expected, he whipped that knife at Snake who jumped back, feeling the knife's razor edge just graze his chin. Dog-man took half a step forward and slammed his revolver into Chastain's head, dropping the little man.

Johnny Simon had his revolver out, searching the crowd, looking to see who would come forward first to defend Chastain. The gambler never went anywhere without armed men protecting him. Simon spotted two men moving fast toward Dog-man, yelled out and fired at one, knocking him to the floor.

Snake spun at the warning and was about to shoot the second man when he gave it up, slipped his weapon back in its holster and bent to help his partner. "Simon? I'm called Snake, this here's Dog-man. We're bringing you a message from the Otter family."

"Snake, eh?" Simon stuck a huge hand out and offered a smile along with it. "You need to be aware that you just made one big enemy. Sheriff will be here any second and for all intents he works for Millard Chastain, the man on the floor bleeding from the head. Let's go out the back door and make it for my place. Hurry now."

Johnny Simon led the way through the mingling crowd, around the end of the long bar, and out the back door. It was a quick walk to the wagon works building. "Saw my cousin, did you? Just about the nastiest woman in Arizona Territory. I do love that lady. She took hold of old Jeremiah ten years ago, dried him out, taught him how to ranch and farm and runs the man ragged."

Snake had to laugh right out, agreeing with every word the big wheelwright said. "We got to their place in time to watch their barn burn to the ground. She said this Chastain feller was responsible. She said you should know. That the same Chastain that Dog-man bashed in the head?"

"Same one, I'm afraid. There were many who saw Chastain pull that knife but there won't be one to admit it. It's gonna be our word against Chastain's, so prepare yourself for some rough going when old Bucky boy gets here."

"Bucky boy?" Dog-man laughed as he asked who that might be.

"Buck Gabbard, Sheriff," Simon said. "Nasty bastard, mean, always on the prod. Best bet, don't show the least amount of weakness." Simon was about to say more when Sheriff Gabbard and the still bleeding Millard Chastain walked into the Wagon Works.

Chastain was not large at all in height and weight, but Gabbard was well above average in both. His weight could almost be considered obese and he wore both a belt and suspenders since he didn't have a waist. He carried a short, double barreled shotgun and had it aimed at Johnny Simon.

"You three, drop your weapons and I mean right now."

"You ain't got no call to ask that, Buck." Simon nodded toward the office door. The old man was standing in the doorway, also carrying a double barreled shotgun. "Might want to ease yours down and talk to us peaceful like. Ain't but one man in this building right now that has broke the law and you're standing next to him."

Chastain straightened up and started to say something but was cut off by Dog-man. "Yup," he said. "Pulled a knife on old Johnny Simon, that outlaw did."

"That's the truth, Buck," Snake said. He made up his mind he would not call the man sheriff but would use the name Buck. "I was standing right there. Saw the whole thing. Be glad to testify to that, too."

Simon had a hard time controlling his chuckle, coughed a bit instead. "That's the truth. This man," and he pointed at Dog-man, "saved my life. Your friend and benefactor was going to carve me up, Bucky." Simon rested his hand on his sidearm and glared at the sheriff. "I think it's time to leave now."

Buck Gabbard knew immediately he had made a mistake coming to the wheelwright without several deputies, knew he couldn't do a thing with three armed men staring him down, and hated Millard Chastain for creating these problems.

"This ain't over, Simon." Gabbard eased the hammers down on the shotgun, all the time glaring at the three men. "You saddle tramps best be out of town by sunset. Don't want your kind around here."

Dog-man couldn't take his eyes off Chastain. *He hasn't said a word or made a move. The kind that would shoot you in the back in half a second. He's already plottin' our demise.* "Our little camp's out of town some, Chastain, in case you're looking for something else to burn down. Didn't do a very good job at the Otter's place."

"You bastard," Chastain howled. He leaped forward, reaching again for his knife. Dog-man's Colt was out and cocked and Chastain pulled up short. "You're a dead man, saddle tramp. Dead, do you hear?" He was screaming right in Dog-man's face.

"Got bad breath, too," Dog-man said and punched the gambler, knocking him to the ground.

Gabbard took a step forward and the old man at the office door simply said, "Don't move, Buck."

"As I said," Johnny Simon said, "it's time for you to take your-selves out of here. No more stupidity, Buck. From you or Chastain. Only one crime has been committed and you know what and who and it ain't none of us did it. Now, get the hell out of here."

***

"Why do these people always think we're saddle tramps, Dog?" Snake and Dog-Man walked Chastain and the sheriff to the wide doors of the Wagon Works and watched them head for the Bordertown

Saloon, Chastain's saloon and gambling hall.

"I guess because we are," Dog-man laughed. "Least, I guess that's what we are." They followed Johnny Simon into the office and found cane back chairs. "Ain't seen a sheriff get intimidated like that in a long while. This gonna come down hard on you, Johnny?"

"More on you two than me. Gabbard protects Chastain's businesses and isn't much worried about so-called crime or street trouble. He'll catch hell from Chastain and work hard to wipe you two off the map." He pulled a box of cigars from a desk drawer and offered them around. Tell me about this fire at Otter's place. That bothers me."

The old man got his pipe lit and found a bottle of whiskey and some tin cups. "Name's Gunderson, Shorty Gunderson." He poured drinks around. "You boys are big targets right now, but you are also heroes to a degree. Ain't too many men in this border town that will stand up to Millard Chastain. Don't let that go to waste."

"Shorty's right," Simon said. "Tell me about this barn burning at the Otter's place."

"We came to that cantina to meet up with you and have some food," Snake said. "Any way we can go back in there without starting a riot or something?"

"Let's do that. I never got my dinner either. You can tell me all about Virginia while we eat. We'll be as safe as anything at Pedro's. He hates Chastain. The gambler came to town and opened Bordertown Saloon and Gambling Hall and has been trying to ruin Pedro's business ever since. Tried to burn him out and that didn't work, then tried to have the sheriff close him down and that didn't work."

"Doesn't sound like this Chastain feller has had the luck of the draw," Snake said. "Pedro must have many friends."

"His friends, including me, put out the fire and went to the city elders to stop the sheriff. The sheriff is supposed to maintain order in the county, but Yuma City Marshal Broderick Caine takes care of town crime. The two don't mix well. Did you notice that only two Chastain men came to the man's rescue? He's not welcome in Pedro's most of the time. You two will be honored guests, I think."

"But this Marshal Caine didn't respond to the shots or dust up either," Snake said. "What are we getting into, Dog?"

20

"I want those men dead, Buck. Dead. You hear me? Dead." Chastain was shaking he was so angry. He and the sheriff were in Chastain's office, just behind the liquor room at the Bordertown Saloon and Gambling Hall. He wiped blood from his head, wondered if any teeth had been knocked loose from the punch to his face.

Bordertown Saloon was remade from an old Spanish garrison stables so that it was a long, low building mostly open to the central plaza. It had an open timber design with tile roofing. Gambling included the regular array of table games and was centered in the building. A drunk or someone not quite proficient in any of the games were fair game to dealers who knew every way to cheat.

Bloody heads or even brutal death came to those who argued. Chastain's dealers had been thrown out of the rowdiest towns in the west. Those that ran the tables on the steamboats were even more ruthless. Sheriff Buck Gabbard protected the operations and City Marshal Caine wouldn't challenge the sheriff.

The bar filled the south part and dining the north. Chastain believed he offered the finest food in Arizona Territory and the fact that Pedro Gonzalez's Cantina out drew Bordertown was a festering boil.

"Nobody treats me like that. You get Ace Shaw and his men and kill those two."

"Ain't seen Ace for a couple of days. Sent him out to burn out Jeremiah Otter, like you wanted, but he ain't come back yet. What do you want me to do with Simon? He's gettin' mighty uppity with you." Subservience was Gabbard's way and he was well paid for the boot licking.

"Him and that old man need to learn their place in this town." Chastain said. He poured some whiskey for the two and let a smile creep across his thin face. "I've always enjoyed a nice warm fire in the evening. Late in the evening."

"Kinda warm this time of the year for one, I expect." Gabbard downed his whiskey and stood up. I'll find Ace right away. Then the dawn spread across the man's face. "Oh, fire. Yeah," he said. "Ace knows about them, too."

"I'd be on my way to New Orleans," Chastain muttered, "if the pickin's weren't so good here." He walked out into the large gambling hall and flagged one of the dance girls over. "Seen Greg Stover today?"

"He's at table two, Mill. Want me to get him?"

"Yeah and bring a friendly lady back to the office with you." She smiled, thinking that would be a quick hundred dollars for an afternoon's work. A mid-day party with the boss was always good for the poke.

Stover was a snarly little back-stabbing cutthroat who did special jobs for Millard Chastain, usually late at night. His specialty was slit throats, but he was also fast and deadly with his handgun. He barged into the office with a dancehall girl on each arm. "Must be something big to get this kind of treatment, Chastain. Your boy, good old Ace Shaw, couldn't get the job done, eh?"

"What are you talking about, Stover?"

"The Otter place, Mill. Only burned the barn down. House is standing tall and pretty at this minute. I've told you about sending out boys instead of men. How about a drink?"

"Tell me, Stover. Now." Chastain sat rigid in his chair, shook off one of the girls trying to rub his scrawny shoulders. "This one of your games?"

"Not my game, Mill. Might be more Buck's style. I rode in this morning and saw the barn rubble but the house was just fine, standing in early morning light. Looks like Jeremiah's wife got the better of you, again." He chuckled almost with a sly threat attached. "She's gonna be the death of you."

"All right ladies, the party's over. Get out," Chastain said. He waited until they scampered out of the office. "I want you to find Buck Gabbard and call him and Ace Shaw off what they should be planning for tonight. Send him down to the river or something." Chastain was having a hard time thinking about getting Johnny Simon burned out after finding that Ace Shaw bungled the Otter attack.

"Put together a small crew and burn down Johnny Simon's Wagon Works. Kill everyone in the place." Anger was replacing thought.

"I thought he was building you some kind of fancy carriage?"

"Was," Chastain murmured. "Watch out for Caine. Better get moving."

***

"I don't know what you're talking about, Stover. What does he mean, go down to the river?"

"I don't know, don't care, Buck. Where's Shaw?"

"Don't know. Haven't seen him since I sent them out to the Otter place."

"That means he ain't coming back, Sheriff." Stover had a broad smile on his normally angry face. "Only burned the barn down, Buck. House is still standing. Now I know why Chastain is so angry. How much did he pay you, Buck?"

"Shut up, Stover. Damn." Buck Gabbard walked off, cussing quietly, wagging his head and could hear the laughter from Greg Stover.

Stover made his way down to the river and into one of the many saloons along the waterfront. "Lookin' for Meany or Louie," he said to a barman.

"Back table," the barman said. Greg Stover moved through the crowd toward the back and spotted the men.

"Lookin' to make a few coins, boys? Got a project for you."

"Depends on the number of coins. Stover and the color," the one called Louie said. Louie was a deck hand on one of the steamboats that plied the river between Mexico and Yuma, and in between voyages did special jobs for Stover, Chastain, or anyone else who might need a fast knife or quick knuckles.

The riverfront was a maze of warehouses, saloons, joss houses and whore houses. Men lived a rough life and many died there without anyone outside the district knowing it. The river was affected by tides coming from Mexico and by the seasons of the north country. The heaviest amount of shipping took place in the late spring and summer because of Rocky Mountain snow melt, thus a river running full.

"Gonna burn out a burr in Chastain's butt," Stover laughed. "Got a couple of double eagles for each of you if you're with me. Maybe a bonus if you kill one of the people who own the place."

"Sounds fair if there's a bottle or two coming with the coins. I got nothing better to do. How about you, Meanie?" Meanie poured a drink, glared at Stover, and grunted something that Louie took as his acceptance. "Good. We're in, Stover."

**

"We should have some kind of plan, Dog. We've got ourselves between a pair of jaws ready to chomp down on us. I think this idea of ours, always helpin' people, ain't our best line of work." The two were camped up about half a mile out of Yuma, in a rocky patch of desert surrounded by bushes and stunted trees.

"Got a nice view of mud that some are calling a river," Dog-man said. "That's California we're looking at on the other side. What are you thinking, Snake?"

"Losing, Dog-man. Until coming from Las Cruces, we were always gaining in some way, whether it be by making friends or finding gold. We haven't gained since leaving Las Cruces. Lost April and those kids and now, it looks like we're gonna lose a chance to ride a big old steamboat. Just cuz a barn burned down."

Dog-man chuckled and leaned back on a rock. "That ain't what's bothering you, old man. What is it?"

"That barn. It's a symbol, Dog. It called us, just like that cattle rancher in Denver or the stage robbery. That gold mine called us. And the Indians attacking April and the kids. We gotta help that family, Dog. Chastain ain't gonna be happy until that family is burned out. We gotta pack up this camp and ride back into Yuma and have another talk with Johnny Simon."

"I thought you said it ain't what we do best. Helpin' people." Dog-man was still trying to hold in a chuckle. "You're replacing April with Virginia Otter, Snake."

"Ain't the first time I've been wrong," Snake muttered. "That sheriff's in my craw, Dog, and that gambler needs a good thrashing. Johnny Simon told us a good deal about him. He wants to rule Yuma but some of the fish can't be corralled. Maybe we should try to meet this Marshal Caine feller."

"We ain't had the best luck with lawmen, Snake. Let's pack up and head back to town. We can settle in at Simon's place. He'll let us stay a day or two, I think. Shorty Gunderson won't argue about having company."

"He'd be the kind of man you want standing behind you with that shotgun," Snake laughed. "Let's get packed."

21

It was almost dark when Snake and Dog-man rode up to the closed gates of the Simon Wagon Works. They could hear work going on inside and used the manway to enter the large enterprise. "Howdy, Shorty," Snake yelled out. "Just me and Dog-man. Don't shoot."

Shorty made the move for his scatter gun when he heard the wrought iron door hinges scraping and eased up. "Gettin' slow in my old age, boys. Should have had you covered before you spoke. Come on in."

"Think Johnny would let us fort up here for a day or two?" Dog-man asked.

"Ask him. He's right in the office there."

It took less than a minute for the deal to be made and the boys brought their animals in and got them settled. "I had it in my mind that you boys would be out of town by now," Johnny said. "Something change your mind?"

"Yup," Snake said. "Just about everything. If we were to go looking for him, where would we most likely find Marshal Caine?"

"Ooh, Snake," Johnny Simon said. "Caine ain't as bad as Buck Gabbard, but he ain't Mr. Sugar either. I'm sure he's heard about the ruckus at Pedro's by now and might be on the prod. He wouldn't worry me, but he might take a chance on busting you two. You might want to save that for morning."

"Good idea," Dog-man said. "Snake gets riled when people get hurt or mistreated and he ain't always nice about it. I'm up for a platter of enchiladas at Pedro's."

The four men walked down the boardwalk to Pedro's Cantina, watching night life unfold on Yuma's central plaza. Mariachi bands were strolling about, dancing couples laughed and made merry, and Mexican and American cowmen strutted in their town best. The evening breeze cooled the desert air, stars shone bright and the nasty smell of the big river went the other way.

Shorty Gunderson led the way into the cantina and found a table near the kitchen. Whiskey, tequila, and beer were brought to the table and orders for great platters of food were given. Pedro made his way through the busy crowd, offering a wide smile.

"Johnny, these are the men who took the knife from Chastain, eh? I wanted to say something when you were in earlier but couldn't break free. You have made a big enemy of that little pimp, but a great friend of me. Welcome to Pedro's."

Snake and Dog-man smiled and nodded to the short but heavy Pedro Gonzalez. "Glad to be here," Dog-man said. Pedro signaled for some strolling musicians to come to the table, bowed slightly, and moved off.

"That's why he's a success," Johnny said. "I thought you were leaving."

"We did too," Snake said. "How bad is the threat to the Otter's? Can't get that burning barn out of my mind. Can't stop seeing those kids with their weapons and their mama with hers. I ain't going nowhere until I know they're safe."

Little eight-year-old Becky became twelve-year-old Geneva that fast and Virginia might yet be called April. "We just spent considerable time with a family that was in the direst of trouble, Johnny. It eats on me when people are taken advantage of." Snake shook his head, took a sip of tequila and washed it down with beer. "She said it was Chastain's men."

"He contracted for large amounts of corn from many of the farmers in the valley," Shorty said, "but never collected the corn nor paid a penny out, either. Lots of money was lost and he says the farmers owe him. It was a poor attempt at controlling the corn market and ruined the market in this part of the territory. Don't make sense to me, but if the farmers don't pay up, he burns them out. Jeremiah Otter is lucky he only lost his barn."

"Chastain will try again," Johnny said. "You can go to the bank on that."

"Where do you fit in, Johnny? Virginia said you were sort of cousins." It was Dog-man's turn to have some tequila and beer and he made a terrible face doing it. "Don't like that stuff. Get some whiskey, Shorty."

"Tequila needs lime, Dog-man," Johnny said. "My father and Virginia's mother are step-brother and step-sister, so that sort of makes us step cousins. We've never really been that close, but with the attack on Virginia's family by Chastain, we are now. I've stayed out of Chastain's shenanigans, but here again, that nonsense today with the knife has changed my mind."

The four were back in the wagon building within the hour. "You live in the building, too?" Snake knew that Shorty Gunderson did, but not Johnny Simon.

"All the comforts of a fine Victorian mansion right behind the office, Snake. A fine dining room, seldom used, a parlor, never used, and a bedroom often used. I plan to use it within the next ten minutes. Good night, gentlemen."

He left amid laughter and Dog-man and Snake headed for one of the stalls to lay out their bedrolls. Shorty had a nook set aside along the north wall and walked that way. "It's been one long day, Snake. Don't wake me until the coffee's ready."

Snake made some noises that weren't words as he slipped into his bed roll and it was a short moment until the noises turned to loud snoring.

***

"You got the kerosene, Meanie? We'll empty it along the outside walls and back into the haystack. Light the hay and it will burn to the building. We'll be in the shadows and shoot whoever comes out to fight the fire."

Meanie just grunted and started pouring kerosene from a five gallon can. He covered the entire east side of the large building and had enough to dribble a line of the flammable liquid to a large stack of dry hay, He emptied the can into the hay and Louie stepped forward with a tin of matches.

"Easiest money I've made in a while," he joshed, dropping a lighted match into the kerosene. The two men ran into the shadows with their rifles, waiting the someone inside to come running.

It was a short wait. Gunderson smelled the kerosene even before it was lit and howled an alarm. He yelled "Fire," over and over, loud enough to get everyone up and in their boots. Snake opened the manway and felt a bullet blow his hat off. "Another way out, Shorty? This door is covered by someone with a rifle."

"This way," Johnny Simon raced in, in time to see Snake jump back from the door. He led the men through the office and into his palatial apartment, to a door at the far back. Simon eased the door open, no shots were fired and the four moved out into the darkness.

The east side of the large building was ablaze and Johnny started to run for one of the fire bells placed around the plaza. Buckets were stacked near cisterns and the bells brought the fire-boys a-runnin'.

"No!" Snake grabbed him just as two bullets slammed into the adobe wall, inches from his chest.

"I see 'em," Dog-man said. He raised his rifle and eased back on the trigger, blowing half of Meanie's head away. Dog-man jacked another round in and watched Louie dive behind some barrels on the ground. "Behind those barrels," he said, and pointed at them. "Go to our right, Snake and Johnny, move left. Shorty, be ready for whoever that is to move and hit him with everything you've got."

"What are you going to do?" Shorty asked.

"Be a target." Dog-man waited until Snake and Johnny were in position and dove into the dirt of the plaza, rolled twice and came up under a wagon. Louie did what Dog-man hoped he would do and tried to get a shot off. Instead, Shorty pumped three shots into his middle and the outlaw tumbled out into the dirt.

Bells were ringing all around the plaza and men were moving fast, setting up the bucket brigades. Two hose carts, pulled by teams of fire-boys raced into the plaza, laying hose from the cisterns to the fire and other running firemen brought hand pumpers. In just minutes, a full attack on the east wall of the Wagon Works building was underway.

"Beautiful to watch, isn't it? They practice and practice and live for this moment," Johnny Simon said. Great streams of water knocked the fire down quickly. "Are both the men dead?"

"No," Dog-man said. "This one ain't got a whole lot of time left, but he's alive."

Before anyone could talk to Louie, City Marshal Caine arrived on the scene. "What's this, Mr. Simon?"

"These men lit the fire, Marshal, then tried to kill us when we ran from the building. I recognize both of them."

"Yeah, me too," Caine said. He was dressed in wool pants, Mexican blouse and an eastern style hat. He carried a shotgun and wore an impressive Colt. Ivory handles, silver inlay tooling and heavy black leather belt and holster. "The dead one's called Meanie and this yahoo is Louie Cannard. Works on one of Chastain's riverboats."

Caine knelt down next to Louie. "Who paid you, Louie? Ain't seein' a doc until you tell me. Who?"

He jabbed a finger into the man's side and Louie,

whimpering, said "Stover."

Caine stood up and motioned for some men to get him to the doctor's. "Greg Stover paid for this, but Stover's got no interest in you, Simon." He turned to Snake and Dog-man. "You the two yahoos got into it with Chastain yesterday?"

"It was us," Snake said. "We ain't yahoos and we ain't saddle tramps. You people down here got no manners."

"Easy, Snake. Don't get him all riled, Marshal. Ain't good for him. This Chastain fool pulled a knife on Johnny Simon and we called him on it."

"I know. I got the whole story from Pedro. Sorry about the yahoo call. Johnny, what do you see here?"

"Chastain, Marshal. Millard Chastain is written all over this. He's clever, though. Had Stover make the deal with these two. Keeps his name out of it. Guess you heard about the Otter place? These two helped Virginia and Jeremiah. These are good men, Marshal."

"So, I've heard," Caine said. "Buck Gabbard wants me to arrest you," he said to Snake. "Don't think I will." He motioned for another couple of men to haul Meanie's body off and walked over to talk with the chief of the firefighters.

"Interesting." Snake watched him go and turned to Dog-man. "Think I like him, Dog."

"I got to get inside," Simon said. The four walked to the front of the building and found the large doors wide open and hoses and men inside. The men were rolling up their hoses and one came up to Simon.

"Got to it quick, Johnny. Outside wall is singed pretty good, but inside looks fine. Didn't open the hoses, so none of your fine wood got wet. You've made your insurance payments, have you?"

"Regular and on time," Simon said. There were three independent fire engine companies in Yuma and businesses paid insurance money to one or others of them, making sure they would respond if you had a fire. It was slow response to a business that didn't have that insurance and led to large bills or no business.

"How do we prove Chastain is behind this?" Dog-man asked. "Knowing it and proving it are two different things."

"We'll need to find Greg Stover," Simon said. "He hangs out along the riverfront most of the time."

"Then that's where we're going," Snake said. "Right after coffee in the morning."

22

"Just heard that Simon's place burned down," Greg Stover said. He was standing at the bar in The Hideaway, unable to hide the satisfaction of those words. The Hideaway was a run-down saloon along Riverside Road and home to some of Yuma's most wanted. "It would be a shame if some of those fancy carriages of his burned up."

"Naw," the barman said. "They caught it in plenty of time. Old Meanie's dead and Louie is all shot up, though." The barman couldn't help seeing Stover take a quick and deep breath. "Two of Simon's friends were there and shot 'em. Heard that Louie spent some time talking with the marshal, though."

Stover tightened up even more at that comment. The barman thought his jaws were tight enough to break a tooth. Stover never said a word, just turned and marched out of the saloon. *I gotta get out of town and quick. Louie is sure to have spouted off. A good kick where it hurts and he'd tell the world all about our deal.* Stover headed for the docks.

"You leavin' out today?" He called to a deck man

on the Columbia.

"Nothing's moving until late tomorrow, Stover. A boat or two coming in later, though."

Stover nodded and walked back toward the long row of bawdy houses. He had his horse tied off behind Kitty's, mounted, and rode up and into Yuma proper. *Chastain's gonna be in a rage, sure as hell. Get my poke and leave out now.* He kept a room above Charley Smith's Market and ran up and grabbed a satchel filled with coins and bills, jacket and bedroll and raced down for his horse.

"Hold it right there, Stover." City Marshal Caine was standing next to Stover's horse, a rifle comfortable in his hands. "We need to have a little talk. Ease all that you're holding to the ground, then slowly loosen that gun belt."

Panic made a dash through Stover, but he fought it off and laid his belongings down in the dust of the busy street. He was looking down the barrel of a Henry as he slowly undid the gun belt and began to let it slip to the ground. He was not as fast as he thought he was, though. Instead of letting the belt fall to the ground, he grabbed the butt of that pistol, pulled it, cocked it on the way out of the leather, and felt the hot sting of lead blowing him back ten feet.

The shock of that spinning chunk of lead slamming into his upper chest made him drop his gun and Caine had it scooped up before the dust settled. Caine saw his shot hit high and to the right on Stover's chest, probably breaking lots of bones. "I ain't gonna let you die, Stover, but you won't ever pull a gun on a lawman again. Might not even have an arm to use on that side." He was snickering as he motioned to a couple of looky-looks to go for the doctor.

The single rifle shot brought bunches of people from businesses and nearby houses and Caine shooed them away. "Nothing to see, men. Just another rat up from the riverfront. Go on back to whatever you were doing." It was less than five minutes and Buck Gabbard swaggered up to the scene.

"What's this, Caine? Shooting another citizen?"

"One of your fine supporters, Sheriff. Mr. Stover here paid a couple of your supporters to burn Mr. Simon's building down and shoot Mr. Simon and whoever was with him."

"Probably can't prove that, Marshal." Gabbard had a nasty smile on his face.

"Well, I don't think Louie's gonna die, Sheriff and he told me all about it." He knew that even if Louie did die, more than one person had heard the confession, and decided to put a little fear into Gabbard's head. "Mentioned several names as a matter of fact."

Gabbard winced slightly at the comment and tried to hide his feelings. *Chastain's gonna have a fit over this. So that's why I was sent away, eh? Chastain thought Stover could do a better job. Better go see that little gambling dandy.*

The doctor drove his buggy right up to Stover's hurting body and stepped down. "Let's get him in the buggy, Marshal. You drive it while I get that bleeding stopped. Go to the mission hospital, not my office. Cannard passed during the night, by the way."

Gabbard pretended he didn't hear the doctor's words and walked on down the street. "Louie's dead and Stover's all shot up," he murmured. "Chastain's gonna be screaming mad."

***

Snake and Dog-man made the quick ride from the center of town to the riverfront district and tied their horses off in front of a wretched looking saloon. "Must be the better part of town, eh Dog?"

"This is worse than anything we found in El Paso, Snake and some of those pleasure palaces were bad, bad. Hope the beer's cold."

"I'm sticking with whiskey. Heard somewhere that it's a good disinfectant." They were chuckling when they walked into the Riverfront Saloon. The barman hadn't smiled in ten years or more and grumbled a good day to them. He was stocky, heavily muscled, and wore a once white apron over what would be working clothes on the docks. Snake couldn't take his eyes off the massive hands the man had.

"Whiskey or tequila? Got no beer today. You the strangers took a knife away from Chastain? Wish I'd see'd that. Well? One or the other?"

"Whiskey," Snake said. *How would he have the slightest idea of who we might be? This is one interesting little town. Everybody knows everything about everybody.* Snake looked over to Dog-man who seemed to be thinking the same thing and smiled. "Heard we might find a feller named Stover down this way. He come in here, does he?"

"Ain't good manners to be asking about people," the barman snarled. "Might have heard the name, maybe not. What's your business, anyway?"

"Heard he's coming up short of men to work for him. Thought we'd check." Dog-man poured whiskey into two slightly used glasses and handed one to Snake.

"I don't think so," the barman said. "I think you're

the two put Louie Cannard and Meanie down last night. You got targets on your backs from lots of different angles right now."

Snake looked at Dog-man, cocked his head slightly, and looked back at the barman. "You run the newspaper here in town, do you?" He got a chuckle out of that. "Seem to know a lot about what we do."

"Seems Millard Chastain be lookin', Buck Gabbard be lookin', and this Stover you're asking about, he be lookin too." There was a hint of a chuckle from the brawny barman and he took the bottle and poured himself a drink, toasting the boys.

"Best find a hole to crawl into, boys, cuz the hunt has started."

"Just how much of this riverfront does Chastain own?" Snake grabbed the bottle back and poured himself and Dog-man a drink.

"What Millard Chastain don't own he controls and that goes for men and whores, too. Don't include me, though. He don't like me and I don't like him. But I ain't no dumb bastard, neither. I pays' him his due, every month and on time, just like those that lick his boots."

Snake took a long drink of his whiskey and tried to put together the puzzle this man laid out. *There's a whole lot more to this man than what we see, but what? Why would he seem to know so much about us? Our best bet is to get the hell out of here before something bad happens.*

Dog-man had been looking around the dark and dirty saloon and realized that they were the only ones in the place. "That why the place is empty? Word put out by Chastain to keep people away?"

"Maybe. Maybe not," the barman snarled. He

poured himself another hit. "It's early."

To Snake, the man seemed to be going out of his way not to be friendly. *Why? You got a saloon in the meanest part of town, where drinking is a natural daily event, why chase off two customers. Maybe because of who we are? But then again, just who are we to worry the man?*

"You'd make some points, then, if you should just happen to let the word out that you know where we are, eh?" Snake had a grand smile on his face and slapped his glass down on the bar. "On the other hand, Mr. Barman, we might spread the word that we learned considerable during our time here."

"You working on something?" The barman said it very quietly. "You're seeing something and I like that. My name's Candy, George P. Candy, Deputy U.S. Marshal, on the sly." His whole demeanor changed as he said that, and a smile slowly spread across his broad, scarred face. "Been working to take Mr. Chastain out of business for some time. Might could use a bit of help from a couple of drifters who seem to have the same idea."

"Well now," Dog-man said. "Just listen to that. Chastain's gonna go down for sure, Snake."

"He is," Candy said. "What's your part in all this? From what I understand you two haven't been in town long enough to even know where to piss."

"Long story, Marshal, but I guess we got time," Snake drawled. *Ha. I got you, Mister Marshal. I knew there was something up.*

"Call me Candy. You two are the only people within a hundred miles who know I'm a deputy marshal and I want to keep it that way. The federal judge in Tucson sent me here and now you know it and why."

Snake spent half an hour describing what happened at the Otter farm, meeting up with Johnny Simon and the attempted burning out of the Simon Wagon Works. "Mr. Chastain has used up all my patience, Candy. He's going to go after Jeremiah and Virginia, sure as I'm standing here."

"One of those men you shot and buried was probably Ace Shaw. He ran a small gang of cut throats and did the bidding of men like Sheriff Buck Gabbard and Greg Stover. That's probably why Stover had to use Louie Cannard and Meanie to burn out Simon. You've put a big dent in the outlaw population around here, Snake." Candy chuckled as he poured another round of whiskey.

"You still haven't told me what your plans are," Candy said.

"Thinkin' we should ride out to Otter's place." Snake slowly shook his head, looked at Dog-man, then Candy. "Want to do a lot more, but that's a start."

"City Marshal Caine is limited, jurisdiction wise and you two need to stay far away from Buck Gabbard. He'll shoot you in the back and call it suicide. Chastain is sure to have money on your heads and there are those in town who need money."

"You said you thought we could help to bring Chastain down. How?" Dog-man asked.

"I think Snake has the right answer. But it puts the Otter family in the same sights that you two are in. If you took up residence at the Otter farm and the word was spread that you were there, all those guns would come looking." Candy was contemplative, got quiet as he paced behind the plank bar. "Sure to put that family in jeopardy."

"More than they already are, I'm afraid," Snake

said. "No, Dog and I need to be there, but we don't need to bring them more trouble."

"I've heard that Virginia Otter is just about the toughest woman in the valley. Why don't you ask her?" Candy did some more pacing. "I've got an ear in Caine's office and have ears at Chastain's saloon and on his boats. I could get a warning to you I think if Chastain made his move."

"It's the 'I think' part that bothers me," Dog-man said.

"I like the idea of letting Virginia and Jeremiah make the decision," Snake said. "Let's ride out there, Dog and get this going. I'm gonna worry myself to death over those kids, though. That little girl is just as tough as her mother."

There he goes. Dog-man looked his partner up and down and saw that he was already at the Otter place, at least in his head. *Those kids are gonna love him half to death just like the Theron kids did. That man has family written all over him and he don't know it, won't accept it when I tell him. What have we got ourselves into this time?*

"If one of you isn't back here in the next couple of days," Candy said, "I'm going to assume you are holed up at the Otter place and spread the word. I've got three men that I can depend on and will come your way fast if I hear anything."

"Glad you're on our side," Dog-man said. Snake coughed some and headed for the door. Candy just stood behind the bar with a smile on his face.

23

Millard Chastain was spluttering angry when the word of Louie Cannard's death reached him. He was in his best livery, silks and satins, finest beaver hat, and ivory handled Remington at his side, but his language was straight from the riverfront. Buck Gabbard stood, almost at attention, facing the angry gambler.

"Word around town is those two saddle tramps headed out of town, riding east. My guess is they're heading for the Otter farm. Ace Shaw and one of his gang has run away, but I can put together some good men to finish what has been started. I'll lead them myself, Mill, so it's done right."

"If it ain't done right, I'll plant you in that pool of mud they call a river, Buck. Ain't been one thing done right around here and I won't stand for anymore. You hear me, Buck? Say it. You'll do this job right or else."

"I'll do it right, Mr. Chastain. I'll do it right." He all but backed out of the Bordertown Saloon office and scampered out of, one of the doors into the sunshine of the plaza. "Trouble is, the man's right," he muttered. His office was across the plaza, near where the old Spanish Alcalde's offices were. "Wish I knew who those two were, just showing up? I wonder." He stood on the board sidewalk, muttering, glaring at passerby, and finally stepping into the cool office.

"Find Lopez and Rodgers," the sheriff said to a deputy lounging by an open window. "Got a little job for us. Be quick about it."

Chastain had followed Buck Gabbard out of the office and now stood near the end of the bar. "Some brandy, Spike. You and that kid of yours up to making some quick, but not easy, money? I got a job that's been needing done for some time."

Spike Tamblin was a wanted killer out of San Francisco's waterfront and his son, called Sonny, was featured on the same posters. City Marshal Caine would swear he never saw any paper on the two. Spike was large and heavy and mean while Sonny, equally large, was cat-like in his moves. Quick and deadly.

"Never hurts to have extra money, Mr. Chastain. The Sacramento is due in from Mexico this evening. Sonny's on it and I'm sure he'll be up for it."

"Do you know Mr. Candy at the Hideaway Bar?" Chastain growled and Spike nodded. "He's been asking too many questions lately, Spike. I think you and Sonny need to give him a final answer. About two hundred dollars worth of answer."

"Each?" Spike had a nasty grin on his face when Chastain nodded. "Consider it done, Mr. Chastain." Tamblin was already spending some of that blood money before Chastain left the building. He had worked for both Gabbard and Stover and was never in favor of how they did things. "There are more refined ways to kill a man than fire," he murmured. "Knives and cleavers have always been my favorites."

***

"Not gonna be easy convincing that woman that we're gonna protect her." Snake was slouched in the saddle, almost sprawled across the horse's rump. "I ain't convinced me, yet. We get ourselves all involved in these things, Dog. Don't know what I might say to that woman."

"You're the talker, Snake. I'm the looker," Dog-man chuckled. "You have a way with women and children. Me and Jeremiah will wait in the barn for the answer."

"Ain't no way to be, Dog. No way to make light of serious stuff." He sat up straight in the saddle and had his eyes glued on the trail. "Them kids need us, Dog."

The final few miles into the Otter farm were quiet ones. Dog-man worried about his partner Snake worried about the kids. "Smoke from the chimney, Snake, so they're all right," Dog-man said.

"For the moment," Snake replied. They rode up the lane toward the farmhouse wondering if they would even be welcomed. "Hope that lady with the shotgun remembers what we look like."

He didn't have to worry about that. It was little Becky who came running out from some sticker bushes. "Snake," she howled. "Is that really you? Look, Jake, it's Snake and Dog-man, come to visit."

Jake made his way out of the bushes and the two ran to the horses. Snake and Dog-man stepped down and were swarmed by the children. "All right, now, let's go say hello to your folks," Snake said. Jake raced ahead to tell Jeremiah and Virginia that they had visitors.

"Hello, boys," Virginia said. She met them from the top of the porch stairs, this time without the shotgun. "See your steamboat, did you?" There was a tinkle of laughter and Snake found himself looking down at his boots again.

"Yup," Snake said. "There's a lot of trouble in Yuma right now and some of it is headed this way. Can we talk some?"

She saw the storm that should have been his face and ushered them into the spacious house. Becky ran to tell her father and Jake pretended to draw on Dog-man. Dog-man scooped him up and tickled him.

"Come into the kitchen, boys. I just pulled some bread from the oven and the coffee's hot." Her smile was generous, but Snake could see the worry in her eyes. "What kind of trouble in Yuma? The kind that would affect us? Like burning us out? I will say we haven't had any unwanted visitors since the fire."

Jeremiah came in and everyone sat around the kitchen table after the children were sent out to play. Snake quickly told about meeting and helping Johnny Simon at the carriage shop, about the shooting and meeting Candy.

"All of this has to do with us?" Jeremiah asked.

"Of course it does," Virginia answered. "My God, Jer, Chastain's already tried to burn us out once.

He'll come here with a vengeance." She turned to Dog-man. "Do you really think that man is a deputy marshal? Do you have a plan?" She had more questions but held them for the time being.

I wonder why? Why are these men willing to help? Why is Chastain still trying to get even with us? Why are we considered a threat to the man? Maybe all these questions are why Jeremiah always says that I am different from every woman he's ever known.

"We want to fort up with you folks for a while, Virginia." Dog-man said. "Seems we've made ourselves enemy number one in Chastain's life, at least according to Marshal Candy. We need a place to hide and you need protection."

"Will they come here looking for you?" Jeremiah asked. "Seems like you're putting us in even more danger."

"Yup," Snake said. "They would be coming for us. Yup," he said again, but with a smile, "we would be putting you in more danger. And, Yup, we would be here to protect you, because they will be coming whether we are here or not."

"Then you rode out here knowing they would come anyway, and just to protect us?" Virginia got up and walked around to Snake and leaned down and kissed him right on the cheek. "That's the nicest thing anyone has ever done for us." She walked behind Jeremiah's chair and stood with her hands on his shoulders, gently rubbing heavy muscles.

"I'm glad you're here and I want you to stay. Ain't got extra rooms, though." *I can't figure those two out. Snake needs a woman and she better be able to produce a lot of kids.* Virginia smiled and grabbed the coffee pot.

"We'd rather sleep out," Dog-man said. "Ain't much for houses and things."

***

Johnny Simon was having an early dinner at Pedro's when a small Mexican girl came to his table. "Hello, Señor Simon. I'm Carmelita, Pedro's niece. He says to tell you bad men will be riding to Otter farm tomorrow night."

She turned and scampered away into the kitchen before Simon could say anything. "Damn," he muttered. He left most of his dinner and headed back to the wagon works, wondering how Pedro would know. Shorty Gunderson met him half-way, almost in a run.

"Read this, Johnny. It was just delivered by one of the boys who work on the steamboats." He handed the envelope to Simon.

"Damn," Simon said, after he read the hand-written note. He folded it and slipped it back in the envelope. "Lock the place up, Shorty, make sure the fires are banked and ride out to Virginia's ranch and help Jeremiah rebuild that barn of his. Snake and Dog-man are already there."

"You comin'?"

"Soon. Take your weapons, old man. It ain't over." Shorty hustled back to the wagon works and Simon headed down to the riverfront, following directions in the note. *Someone named Candy at the Hideaway bar has information about my cousin and Snake and Dog-man? That trouble is on the way and he needs to see me immediately? Who the hell is this Candy?*

Johnny Simon was a master wagon maker, fine wheel wright, wonderful blacksmith, but was not a deep thinker. He could not fathom why a barman along the riverfront would even know he had a cousin named Virginia. It was a long walk down to the docks and he pulled that note out twice before finding the Hideaway bar. *I don't understand.*

"I'm looking for a man named Candy," he said. "I'm Johnny Simon, wagon maker."

"I know you, Johnny Simon. I'm George P. Candy. Please, let's take a table and have a little chat." There wasn't a soul in the saloon, Johnny noted, as Candy shut but didn't lock the doors. *Haven't seen a feller this big in a long time.*

"That was quite a fight you and your friends had the other night. Came out right too," Candy said. "You prefer whiskey or tequila?"

"Uh, tequila, I guess," Johnny said. "Just what is this all about? Who are you? Why do you even know who I am?"

"It makes me feel good that you don't know," Candy said with a smile. "Snake and Dog-man know and so does your cousin, now. Millard Chastain will know very soon, I hope." He sat down with a bottle of tequila and two glasses. "I'm Deputy U.S. Marshal Candy, Johnny, working for the federal judge in Tucson. I'm here to put Chastain in prison and I need a little help. Snake and Dog-man are in. How about you?"

Before he could answer two men barged through the doors and up to the bar. "You open or not? Ain't never seen the door closed." The older of the two said. "Whiskey, and let's not be slow about it." Spike

Tamblin stood menacingly at the bar, his son Sonny giving Johnny Simon a look over.

Candy got up slowly, eyeing the two and walked back behind the bar. Without saying a word, Candy handed a bottle and two glassed to Spike. He started to go around, then turned back. "I believe you're a barman at the Bordertown Saloon, aren't you? Spike, right?" Candy's right hand had a grip on a club he kept under the bar. There was a shotgun down there, too. "What brings you down here? Don't get many Chastain workers."

"Need to have a little private talk, Candy." Spike turned to Simon, let his hand nurse the handle of his revolver. "Get out. This is private."

Simon saw Candy give just a slight nod of his head and stood up. "Candy and I were having a private little conversation as well. Maybe you'd like to wait your turn." Spike Tamblin pulled iron but before he could fire, he caught a glass full of tequila in the face. He couldn't see, was yelling out in pain and just started pulling the trigger.

Simon danced off to the side, had the bottle in hand and slammed it across Spike's head, knocking the big man back toward the bar. He used the broken neck of the bottle to slash Spike in the face, and on his hand holding the gun, which Spike dropped immediately.

Blood was running freely and Simon took full advantage of Tamblin's inability to see, hammered him two or three times in the head, pummeled the flailing outlaw again and again, until Tamblin fell to the floor, unconscious.

When Spike made his move to draw down on Johnny, Sonny moved to pull his gun only to be looking down the wrong end of Candy's shotgun. "Your choice, Sonny. Do it or don't." Candy watched Sonny slowly relax and pull his hand away from his gun. "Good boy. Now ease that smoker out and put it on the bar. Thumb and finger only."

Sonny Tamblin saw his father, almost unconscious, bleeding heavily, sink to the floor and eased his sidearm out of the holster. He laid it on the bar and stepped back, glaring, first at Candy, then at Johnny. "You're gonna pay for this. Chastain's gonna kill you both."

"Chastain ain't got it in him, Sonny." Candy found a coil of rope behind the bar and threw it at Sonny. "Tie Spike up tight, boy. Johnny, you got a gun?" Johnny shook his head and Candy threw Sonny's pistol to him. "Don't be afraid to use it."

Candy walked around from behind the bar, shotgun in hand and locked the door. He watched Sonny tie up Spike and when he was finished, slammed the butt of the scattergun into Sonny's head, knocking him out cold. "Watch 'em close, Johnny while I tie up Sonny boy here."

The Tamblin men were moved to a storeroom behind the bar, Candy made sure the ropes were as tight as possible and the two walked back to the bar. "This makes it a little easier," Candy said. "Did you ride down here?" Johnny shook his head. "Well, they won't be looking for you right now. Chastain's forces are spread mighty thin." He wanted to light out right away for the Otter place, wanted Simon alongside, but Simon's horse was uptown at the Wagon Works. *What am I thinking?*

"I've got a horse out back. Grab the best of the Tamblin's horses and we'll ride out to the Otter place together. I just hope that Chastain himself will be making the attack on Otter."

"I've never taken another man's horse," Johnny said. "This makes me an outlaw," he murmured.

"No," Candy laughed. "We just be borrowing it. I'm sure I heard Sonny say something about taking care of his horse when we tied him up." Candy laughed but Johnny Simon was still frowning as they walked out of the bar. Johnny took a fine buckskin tethered in front of the bar and Candy went around back to saddle his horse. "Just gonna leave those boys, Candy?"

"Chastain will send someone around when they don't report back. Maybe later today. Maybe tomorrow," he laughed. "We'll just walk the horses through town and then ride hard to Otter's." Candy told Simon about the possible attack on the Otter's, about Snake and Dog-man being there and Johnny told Candy about sending Shorty out after getting his message.

24

Millard Chastain's anger was over the boiling point when he found Buck Gabbard sitting in the sheriff's office. "You really don't know where Ace Shaw is, do you? You sent him to burn out that Otter woman and haven't seen him since, have you? She is the one who has refused to pay for that corn, has mocked me and has brought in those two saddle tramps to fight me. I wonder if she's the reason you don't know where Shaw is?"

Chastain pulled a flask from an inside pocket of his frock coat, took a long pull on it, and did not offer any to Gabbard. "I'm riding out there, Sheriff and I want you and at least three other men to ride with me. You make damn sure they are wearing badges. The Otter family will be arrested for conspiracy or something, and when they try to escape, they will die. You understand me, Buck?" He pulled the flask again and took a long pull.

"This time, Buck, everything they own will burn and everyone there will die." He shook his fist at the sheriff. "We leave in half an hour. No one mocks

Millard Chastain, Buck. No one." Chastain turned
and swaggered out of the office and across the vast
plaza of the old town to the Bordertown Saloon,
leaving Gabbard sitting at his desk, questioning
what was happening.

Chastain's thoughts centered on Virginia Otter
as he prepared for the coming journey. *She knows
too much. I should never have let her know how the
corn deal was to work. All she had to do was make
her payment. I told her it would be kicked back, but
she had to blab it all out to the other farmers and I
lost all that money.* He was almost talking to himself
when he reached the bar.

"Where's Spike? Isn't he supposed to be on duty?"

"Didn't show up, Mr. Chastain. No word at all."
Sam poured a shot of whiskey for Chastain. "Not
like him. Not at all like him."

"No, it isn't, Sam," Chastain muttered. Did Spike
have trouble with that man Candy? Or is he dispos-
ing of the body? Chastain's mind knew that either
way would be trouble coming, too, if Spike wasn't
able to finish the man off. "If I say the name Candy,
do you know who I'm talking about?"

"Yeah, owns the Hideaway bar down on the riverfront. Real pigsty from what I've heard."

"Spike was supposed to meet with this Candy
at the Hideaway. You take one of the men with you
and find him. Better be well armed," Chastain said.

Chastain grumbled something else and headed
back to his office, returning in minutes, carrying
a shotgun. He walked to the stables behind the saloon and saddled up. "Too many things not working
right," he mumbled, riding out to meet with Gabbard and what men he could find.

"It's five miles, boys and a nice paycheck if you do your job. Gabbard, when we get there, I don't want no arguments, no talk. Place the entire family under arrest and at their first move, kill 'em. We'll burn the place to the ground with the bodies inside the house."

"What about those kids?" one of the deputies said.

"They are just as guilty as that witch of a mother," Chastain said. "Kill 'em."

The three deputies looked around, at each other, at Buck Gabbard, at Chastain. Sheriff Gabbard had done some horrible things at Chastain's bidding before, but murdering children? "That ain't right," one of them grumbled and Chastain turned on him, the shotgun aimed at his midsection.

"You will do as you're told, or I'll blow you right in two where you stand. You wear that badge and you will kill that family or I will kill you. I hear one more stupid comment and I start shooting. Let's ride, Buck."

***

"Two riders coming up the drive," Snake said. He and Dog-man were in a small grove of trees on a slight rise slightly west of the lane leading into the farm. "It's Johnny and Marshal Candy. We got us quite a little army, Dog." Shorty Gunderson had arrived several hours before and was with Jeremiah near the burned-out barn.

"Glad you could make the party," Dog-man said. "Think Chastain will hit today? Shorty and Otter are up at the barn, Virginia and the kids are at the house and she has her shotgun and we're down here."

"Good defense," Candy said. "He'll hit today. I know it. He won't wait." He stepped down from his horse, grabbed up his rifle, and handed the reins to Johnny. "Put the horses up, Simon and take a position with Virginia. I'll stay here with these two. If shootin' comes to shootin', let's remember where everybody is."

Dog-man led Candy and Snake back to the scrub trees. "How well do you know Chastain, Marshal? You seem to be able to anticipate his moves."

"Been on his tail for some time, Dog-man. He's been running crooked gambling here and on the river for several years, but it was when he started defrauding the local government, rigging commodity prices and killing people that I became involved. His schemes have cost the lives of two families, complete families, forced the sale of a dozen or more farms."

"You mean killed mother, father, and kids when you say complete families?" Snake was tensed, his eyes blazing, his heart aching. Hurt grown people, well, that happens. Hurt kids and Snake will hurt back. "He tries to hurt these little ones here and he dies, Candy. He dies hard."

"Tell me about the forced sales," Dog-man said.

"Well, with the corn conspiracy, the farmers were faced with a crop they couldn't sell and were forced to sell their farms. You can guess who they sold them to. Rock bottom prices, too." Candy looked Snake right in the eye. "In some cases the farmers were making too much noise, saying too much in public and Chastain would burn them out and leave the bodies." He found some shade and sat down.

"I'd rather not kill Chastain, Snake, if we don't have to. He has people in the territorial and local government that help him and we want those names. If at all possible, I want the man alive."

"Then keep him away from those kids," Snake said. "Will he be showing up with a large group of men? We need to be in a better place if he does."

"You and Dog-man reduced his gang considerably," Candy laughed. "I'm sure he'll bring Gabbard and some of his deputies. He likes to try to make his raids look like they are legal in some sense. Gabbard is a slur on the word lawman and licks Chastain's boots regularly. He's dangerous because he does what he's told."

"Have we got time to have a quick get together with everyone?" Dog-man asked. "Does Shorty Gunderson and Jeremiah know what might be coming at them? Does Virginia know she has to keep those kids safe? We got a lot to protect here, Marshal."

"I know," Candy said. "Johnny is sure to have told Shorty what to expect and is with Mrs. Otter. I'm sure everyone is fully aware, Dog-man, but you are right about our position out here. We're too far from that lane. We need to be much closer to the house and almost right on the drive."

They grabbed their rifles and started down the rise toward the house. "There's some thick brush the kids play behind to scare someone coming in," Snake said. "Got us, they did. Remember, Dog?" He chuckled and pointed at some scrub brush full of needle-sharp thorns, but thick enough for them to hide behind.

"Within twenty-five yards or so of the house, too,"

Candy said. "Let's try to stay several feet apart and if shootin' starts, watch out for shootin' into the house. Buck Gabbard's a fool and Chastain is a hot-head, so there's sure to be shootin'."

***

"There's just so much I don't understand, Johnny." Virginia and her cousin were seated at the kitchen table with hot coffee. Jake and Becky were at the front windows watching for riders. "Chastain expected Jeremiah to go along with his plan to control the price of corn and when that failed, he created a financial disaster for the farmers in the valley. What drives a man like that?"

"Just plain old greed," Johnny said. "Same reason he runs crooked gambling. He doesn't have to be crooked. Gambling odds are in favor of the house to start with, but he wants more than that. And of course, power. Strut around and be called Mister, demand this, demand that, and it gets done. Force people to do your bidding. He'll cheat, lie, do anything, anything at all, to get his way."

Johnny Simon sat back and took a deep breath. "Millard Chastain also takes pleasure in hurting people. He enjoys hurting horses, dogs, his own workers. He's an evil man, Virginia. We have to talk about what to do when he and his gang arrive. Those kids are too willing to get involved in the fight."

"With axes and pitchforks they did a good job on Snake and Dog-man," she laughed. "You're right, though. Let's bring our coffee out front."

Jake had a chair moved so he sat in front of one of the large windows in the living room while Becky was on her knees in front of another window. "Snake, Dog-man and somebody else are hiding in our bushes, Mama," Becky said. "Who is that other man? Is he supposed to be here?"

Johnny Simon noticed that Becky had a double-bladed ax on the floor next to her and had to smile. *Just like Snake said. These kids are a whole lot tougher than I was at that age. My, god, we have got to protect them. I have not been a good cousin to this family.*

"That other man, Becky, is Deputy United States Marshal Candy," Simon said. "I've never seen a bigger man and he can fight. When we see riders coming in, you children have to get back from the windows. Your mama and I will need to be there with our big guns. You need to hide behind the furniture when bullets start flying."

"I want to help," Jake said. He too had an axe next to him. "Mama says we have to protect what's ours. We didn't save the barn, but Papa says because we yelled at those men, we saved the house."

"You did, indeed," Virginia said. Half her face tried to smile, the other half was shrouded in fear, tears were running down her cheeks, not from crying, but from pride. "I'm so proud of you two. You hide behind the furniture and if men try to invade the house, you attack them with your axes."

Johnny Simon recoiled at the thought of telling children to attack men who had guns but had to admit that if men made it into the house, it meant that he and Virginia were probably already dead. "Your mama and I will do everything we can to keep that from happening," he said.

25

"You lead us in, Buck, with your deputies alongside. Arrest them first, let them make a move of some kind and kill every single one of them." Chastain planned to ride behind the group, just in case it went wrong. So many things had gone wrong. *Gabbard might try to not let me down, but he hasn't been good at it lately. If this goes wrong, I gotta get back to Yuma fast.*

As they neared the lane leading to the farm, they could see the remains of the burned-out barn, but not the line-up of horses, saddled, ready for a chase. The large, rambling farmhouse was spread out on a knoll, overlooking vast acreage and open desert. *This isn't right.* Deputy Sheriff Tomas Garcia Lopez had shot or knifed more than one man in his short life, but the idea of killing children was something he would not do.

They turned into the lane and Buck Gabbard pulled his rifle from it scabbard. "We'll ride straight to the house and call them out. Have your weapons ready. They don't have to actually try to escape, if they even argue, kill 'em." He tried his best to sound mean, like Chastain. He and Lopez were on the right and two other deputies were to their left. Chastain, Gabbard noticed was twenty yards or more behind them.

***

"Here they come," Candy muttered. "Chastain is lagging back. He'll run at the first shot, so let's let them ride on by before we make our move. Don't want to lose that man."

"Don't want them too close to the house," Snake said. He held his rifle, cocked and ready and watched Buck Gabbard and Lopez ride right on past him. Chastain seemed to hold back even more, but finally rode by. "Easy now," Snake muttered, bringing the rifle up. He aimed for Chastain's horse just as Marshal Candy pulled down on Deputy Lopez.

"Hold it up, right there," Candy said, standing up, aiming the rifle at Lopez. Snake stood up, about to shoot Chastain's horse, and Dog-man stepped around the stand of thorny bushes, his rifle aimed at Gabbard.

The deputy to Gabbard's left had his rifle at the ready and fired without aiming, blowing a branch off a bush and into Dog-man's face. Snake shot Chastain's horse and Candy shot Lopez in the leg, knocking him to the ground.

Gabbard saw Dog-man fall to the ground, saw Lopez go down, and spurred his horse toward the house, followed by the two deputies. Candy killed one deputy and Snake knocked the other off his horse with a single shot from his rifle. In the melee,

Chastain grabbed Lopez's horse and made a dash for the main road.

"Chastain's running," Dog-man hollered. He took two shots, missing and Snake tried a long shot, knocking Chastain's hat off, but not drawing blood. Candy made a run for Gabbard, grabbing hold of the sheriff and ripping him out of the saddle. All of Candy's size and strength came into play, rolling the horse to the ground as well.

Shorty Gunderson saw Chastain make his get-away and ran for the horses. He was in the saddle fast, galloping off the brow of the knoll toward the action near the bushes. Snake ran out and stopped him. "I'm making this chase, Shorty," he said. Shorty baled off and Snake jumped on, putting spurs to the horse.

Dog-man, bleeding from the thorny branch that had hit him, raced up the hill for the horses and ran at a full gallop toward the main road. "You ain't gettin' all the glory, Snake," he howled, only seeing a cloud of dust in front of him.

Five miles at a full gallop still takes a long time and Chastain had a sizable lead. Snake could see dust, but it was far ahead. *If he reaches town before I can catch him, he probably has a hundred places to hide.* Snake's mind was working as fast as his horse was running and he tried to think where a man as desperate as Chastain was would head.

"He's going for the riverfront," Snake said it right out. "One of those steamboats would be my bet." He had to laugh. "Oh, yeah and all those who work for him populating the saloons ready to defend the boss. You better catch up, Dog. I'm gonna need you."

He was on the outskirts of Yuma and had to

ride through the town, but could tell from those on the street, that someone else had been there first, someone racing as fast as he was. He made for the docks, could feel his horse running out of breath and let it slow down.

"You better be behind me, Dog," he muttered, making his way down through heavy riverfront traffic to the docks. There were two steamboats tied up, but one was getting ready to make way. "Gonna make my first steamboat ride, I think." The Yuma Queen was building steam, people with trunks were loading and cargo was still being loaded as well.

Snake jumped from the horse, got it tied off and was walking fast toward the steamboat just as Dog-man stepped alongside. "Going somewhere, are we? Mexico, perhaps? Guaymas, Mexico?"

"About time you got here," Snake said. "I'm pretty sure Chastain's on that boat but I haven't seen him. What do we do, just walk on board?"

"With the exception of passengers, every person on that boat works for Chastain and he knows what we look like. Can't just walk on, Snake." They were standing near the bow and Dog-man yelled up at a deckhand. "When are you pulling out?"

"Ridin' out with the tide. About dark," The man hollered down. "Got the boss on board, so we'll steam on time."

"Answers that," Snake laughed. "Now, back to question one. How do we get on board and not be recognized by the boss?"

"Question two, Snake, what do we do if we get on board? We ain't lawmen, surely can't try to hold the man. We're in a fix, Partner." Dog-man saw the deck hand watching them. "Any stops along the way?"

"No. Straight to the gulf and on to Guaymas and some of the best food in Mexico."

Dog-man waved his thanks and he and Snake walked across the docks toward one of the many saloons spread out. "Some beer, some chilies and beans and some planning, Dog." Snake led the way. "We could use an army right about now."

The saloon looked out across the dock and they watched the loading as they pondered the questions. "Something going on," Snake said. He nodded toward where a knot of people were congregated. "That's Chastain." They watched Chastain walk down off the boat with at least five members of the crew, each carrying a rifle or shotgun.

"He's going somewhere. Better get back to the horses." Snake took two quick spoons full of beans and chilies, sloshed half his beer down and they moved out of the cantina and toward their horses. "He's got the army, Dog, not us. He's got five well-armed people with him. I wonder where he'll lead us?"

"As soon as we find out we got to find that marshal. He could just be getting stuff to take with him on the boat." Dog-man saw that all five of the boat workers were carrying shotguns or rifles. "Lots of protection there."

"Ride for the Otter place, Dog and tell Candy what we've found. I'll stick to Chastain and try to leave some kind of trail for you to follow. We've got several hours before sunset if Chastain's planning to be on that boat."

"No arguments here," Dog-man said. He stepped into the saddle and rode back up toward town. Snake stood alongside his horse and watched the steamboat hands stand in a group, surrounding their boss. Before long a well-appointed carriage with four-up appeared and everyone boarded.

"Man travels in style," Snake muttered. He followed the carriage away from the docks, anticipating it heading for the Bordertown Saloon, but it didn't. "Gonna get a tour of the town, I think." They bypassed the center of Yuma and took a road that led north along the banks of the river. "Hope Dog recognizes this," he murmured as he tied a ribbon of material from his shirt to a spiny bush.

***

Dog-man rode the five miles back to the Otter place at a solid trot and found Candy in a deep discussion with Buck Gabbard. Dog-man could tell it was a serious talk by the way Candy held his pistol against Gabbard's head. "Snake's tailing Chastain and it looks like the man will be leaving out tonight on one of his steamboats. He has five armed men with him."

"Good," Candy said. "Snake has the favorable odds, but we should give him some help." Candy called Johnny Simon and Gunderson over. "Let Jeremiah Otter keep Gabbard and the wounded deputies here, trussed tight, and we'll ride for Yuma."

"I'll tell him," Johnny said. He ran up to the house and was back with Jeremiah and Virginia in minutes. Becky and Jake came along, too, with their axes. "Gabbard ain't going nowhere," Simon chuckled.

Candy explained what Snake was doing and Dog-man took the time to tell what they had seen and heard on the riverfront. The four men rode in spurts of trotting and walking across the Mohawk Valley, since Dog-man's horse had already made the trip three times and was more than tired. "This old boy won't be getting involved in a hard chase, boys, so if Chastain runs, he's all yours."

As they moved into Yuma, Dog-man spotted a shredded sleeve of a shirt hanging from some brush. "That's Snake's shirt," he said. It was where a road turned north from the main road, and they turned to follow. "I'd know that old shirt anywhere. Know where we're going, Candy?"

"Several ranches along the river that Chastain now owns, following the corn conspiracy. If he's planning on a riverboat trip he probably has cash and incriminating papers hidden somewhere. Probably why he has armed guards with him. Those are the Laguna Mountains in front of us. The ranches are right on the river, so we'll find him between here and the mountains."

They were moving through rough country, every bush had spines, every rock had something that stung, or bit attached to it and every eye was on country inland from the river. "Hard country for cattle and people," Gunderson said. "Johnny brings his wagons, carts, and carriages out here to give 'em a shake down. If they survive this, they'll survive anything."

"Ain't that bad," Johnny laughed. He was about to say something when a series of gunshots could be heard, maybe a mile off. The group moved at a fast lope toward the noise.

"Sounds like Snake's got a war started. Better hurry if we want to be in on the fun," Candy said. They moved over a rise in the desert floor, could see the muddy Colorado on their left and heard more gunshots go off in front to their right. A stand of trees indicated a ranch site and dust told the tale of animals running.

"That dust is coming right at us," Johnny said.

"So is the gunfire," Candy barked. "Take cover, boys. It looks like Snake has them on the run and right at us."

They let the horses stand and found what cover they could, behind rocks, rises in the desert floor, and under those damn spiny bushes. The four-horse carriage was coming down the roadway at a thunderous gallop, one man well behind and moving just as fast. One man was driving the carriage and the others were trying to fire shotguns and pistols at Snake, but he was holding back out of range.

"Drop the horses," Candy yelled as the carriage came on them fast. "If he makes it back to town, we'll have hell breaking him out."

The fusillade was furious, and the two teams collapsed, upsetting the carriage, flinging men and guns into the dirt and dust. Millard Chastain crashed hard into the dirt, rolled, and was on his feet, revolver in hand. Candy's horse was just feet from the wreck and the outlaw was in the saddle in moments, kicking the beast into a gallop.

"There he goes," Dog-man yelled. Snake rode through the debris of the wreck while Candy grabbed a free horse and jumped on board, yelling for Dog-man to take prisoners. Dog-man had already found a horse and was in the saddle, racing to catch up.

"That leaves us," Johnny Simon said to Shorty Gunderson. Let's gather their guns first, then figure out what to do with them."

"If any are still alive," Shorty said. "These are some of the meanest men on the waterfront, Johnny. I recognize three of them from the group that collects from those that owe Chastain gambling or other debts. Any that are alive need to be tied tight."

***

Snake was slowly catching up to the fleeing Chastain and also noted that Candy and Dog-man weren't too far behind. "Come on, boy," he urged his horse. "Let's take this bandito down." They were coming up to the junction where Snake left part of his shirt and Chastain turned down hill and onto the waterfront. Snake was less than twenty-five feet behind and spurred the horse faster.

People along the riverfront watched as Snake leaped from his charger and took Chastain right off his horse. They hit the ground in a heap and Snake was about to bash Chastain's head in when he was hit by something hard and fell, almost unconscious to the dirt. Two men hustled the outlaw to his feet and ran him toward one of the buildings while other men stood outside the doors, guns drawn and cocked.

Snake was groggy, blood-streaked and was having a hard time getting to his feet. He saw Chastain being led away, soon to be out of reach, but couldn't get his legs under him. Candy and Dog-man raced to help get Snake on his feet and watched helplessly as an armed mob moved Chastain down the waterfront to the Yuma Queen, that large steamboat standing ready to depart.

"Damn it," Candy said. "If he gets on that boat,

we've lost him and we can't fight our way through the mob he'll have surrounding the boat."

"We can burn it," Snake said. "That's what he'd do." He tied the other sleeve of his ripped-up shirt around his bleeding head. "That's what he does best. Burn him and his boat, just as he tried to burn out the Otters." Dog-man took in a breath.

He's gettin' riled and that means a lot of trouble for Mr. Chastain. Probably us, too. "Don't get yourself all riled, Snake. It ain't good for our health. Burn that boat? Sure would chase him back to the riverbank, though."

"How do we get close enough? Everyone you see here supports the fool." Candy was shaking he was so angry.

"Gotta be lots of kerosene and tar around," Dog-man said. "Gotta be small boats close by. They won't expect an attack from the river side. The three of us should be able to do a lot of damage."

"And you call me a poet," Snake laughed. "Find a boat, Candy, We'll find the fire starter."

"There's a small pier that way," Candy said, pointing north. "I'll have a boat waiting for you." He took off at a sprint. There was a small boat pulled up on the bank, probably used for fishing and its oars were there. The big man had a struggle but got it into the water and was waiting for the boys.

It was coming sunset as Snake and Dog-man worked their way along the back sides of the buildings and found half a dozen partially filled kerosene cans and brought them to one of the finger piers on the north end of the riverfront.

"Damn cans make enough noise to wake the dead," Dog-man grumbled. He was trying to hold three of them, his rifle and run through the quickly darkening alleyways.

"Don't need to worry none about that with all the noise from the street. Lots of people getting ready to board the steamer."

Candy had the rowboat tied off and by the time they were ready to move off, they had emptied all the kerosene cans and had three full five-gallon cans of kerosene. "We got enough oil to light the whole territory," Snake said.

"Getting dark fast, boys." Candy was quick and strong with the oars and they were in the middle of river, far from the Yuma Queen. "How are those torches coming?" Candy was using his hulk to move the boat through the river, using the current and was using the oars to move them right up to the big boat. "I'll get us close as I can," he hollered.

"Got four good torches," Dog-man said. When you row us alongside the boat we'll spill as much kerosene as we can along the deck, then throw the torches, she should catch right away."

"As long as we ain't seen," Snake said. "When that fire starts, Chastain will be the first one off, you know."

"Damn," Candy snarled again. "One of us has to stay and keep track of that fool."

"Not if we get the fire going before they shove off," Dog-man said. "They'll be too busy fighting the fire to get underway, so it won't matter if he's onboard or not. At least we'll know he ain't heading for Mexico."

What the hell are we doing? Snake was in the bow of the small boat heading toward the steamboat Yuma Queen helping Dog-man soak the torches. Candy was bringing them alongside the big steamboat. *Chastain owns most of the criminal element in this town and we're in this fight because of a family we've never met before. Got no real business being here.*

It was at least ten minutes before they could come alongside the steamboat. She was still tied off, people were still coming on board, but Snake could see armed men watching the waterfront closely. *They ain't watching out here on the water. Just like Dog said.*

Candy used the oars to jockey the dingy as close to the big boat as he could, shipped the oars, stood and grasped the gunnels. He pulled the small craft along the side of the Yuma while Dog-man and Snake poured gallons of kerosene onto the deck.

"Okay," Candy said. Snake and Dog-man lit the torches. "Push off and throw those torches. Let's get the hell out of here."

Dog-man threw the first torch and Candy and Snake followed immediately. They arched, through the night sky and when they hit the deck, the boat lit up as if on display. The fourth torch added to the maelstrom and it wasn't long before screams of terror filled the night air.

Candy was rowing with the current and they made for safety. Men on board the steamboat were shouting orders, women were screaming, and no one, it seemed, saw the little boat with three men making their get-away. Candy followed the current to the last finger pier and they got the boat tied off.

"Time to see if we can find Mr. Chastain." Candy had a big smile on his normally angry face. "Not a shot was fired, boys. Right now, they don't know how that fire got started but it's sure they won't shove off now. Let's find that outlaw gambling man and get some chains on him." Candy was as excited as a ten-year old as he and the boys jumped onto the dock.

"Could sure go for a cold beer right now," Snake said, rubbing the welt along the back of his head. "And find the man that did this." They threaded their way through crowds of people making their way to the docks.

"Are you sure what we just did was right?" Snake was shaking his head, watching flames spit ash hundreds of feet in the air. "What if someone on that boat dies? Dog, we ain't never done nothing like this before." Snake couldn't get it out of his head that they really had no particular reason to even be there. "We ruined a big steamboat, put a lot of lives in jeopardy, just catch an outlaw. Damn."

They were running for their horses through a gathering crowd and Dog-man had more of his mind on getting out of there than contemplating the more serious thought of killing some innocent person on board the boat. "If we get out of here with our skins and hair we'll talk about that Snake."

A spectacle such as a steamboat burning to the water just as night fell was something everyone in Yuma wanted to see. Men, women and children filled the streets hampering the various fire companies responding to the alarms. It was a holiday spirit that seemed to take hold.

They found their horses still tied where they left them. "Let's ride along the riverbank," Candy said. "Ain't no use trying to fight a crowd like that. I think it's time to find City Marshal Broderick Caine. Not sure he's really a straight shooter but we need help."

26

Shorty Gunderson and Johnny Simon did their best to doctor the injured and wounded men who guarded Chastain and watched as night came on. "We're miles from town, Shorty and no food. Got any of your ideas working?"

Shorty had been with Johnny a long time and the men were more friends than employer/employee. "I'm stumped right now, boss. But we do have one horse. I'll stay with these yahoos while you ride back and bring a wagon out. Leave the water, though."

"Look at that," Simon said, pointing toward Yuma. "Something big is burning hot, Shorty." The night sky was ablaze, even from several miles away, they could see tongues of fire dancing and billows of heavy smoke.

"Think Snake and Dog-man had anything to do with that?" They were laughing as Johnny stepped into the saddle for the ride into town. He rode to his warehouse and got the big doors open.

He had a team harnessed quickly and drove a fine wagon into a melee of excitement in the old town. He was amazed at the size and intensity of the large fire raging along the riverfront. The plaza and the streets were clogged with fire companies racing toward the fire. The streets were also filled with men, women, boys and girls, as they moved in swarms toward the inferno, interfering with the fire boys and their apparatus.

It was slow going, moving as best he could toward the road north. He noticed men breaking windows and doors of businesses, using the dockside catastrophe as an excuse to rob and steal from the local merchants. "Bastards," he muttered. "Need to be shot. How low can you get?"

When he reached the intersection and moved north on the now vacant roadway, he stepped the team into a nice trot, making the few miles to Shorty in good time. "Whatever's burning at the docks is bringing the whole town to see," he said as Shorty took the lead rope and held the team. "If it's one of the steamers, she'll burn to the water line for sure. How are things here?"

"We got three dead ones, one almost dead, and one with two broken legs and a mean temper. He's also got a sore head, now. It wasn't the right time to say what he did about my family. What do we do with them, Johnny?"

"Hell if I know. Just drive right up to the Border-town Saloon and drop 'em off, I guess," he laughed. "For real, Shorty, I don't know."

"Candy, Snake, and Dog-man are chasing Chastain and I'd bet they are responsible for that fire," Shorty said. "Bet you big bucks they'll come looking for us at the Wagon Works."

"You're probably right." They got the bodies and

the injured men in the wagon and Shorty drove back to Yuma. "Sure hope Pedro's is open. I ain't had nothing to eat all day, Johnny."

By the time they got back to town, the crowds had diminished considerably but the looting and destruction had not. "Rabble!" Johnny Simon was furious as they neared his big business. He had left the doors open riding out and as Shorty drove the wagon into the building, they found half a dozen men taking tools, fine wood and metal.

"You thieving bastards," Johnny yelled out. He brought his shotgun up and fired off one barrel, not at the men but close enough to cause a stampede. The thieves dropped what was in their hands and raced for the open doors. Johnny let fly with the second barrel at their feet as they raced into the night.

Shorty couldn't hold in the chuckles watching the display, saw Johnny Simon reload the big fowling piece, and started unharnessing the team. "Doubt if you lost much, boss, but they'll be talking about this for a while. I recognized a couple." Johnny just grunted.

They got the injured men out of the wagon and tried to get them settled in a bed of wood shavings. The dead ones were laid out and covered with a sheet of canvas. "Stay sharp with that shotgun of yours, Shorty. I'm going to find Marshal Caine. He can take custody of these fine citizens and maybe he'll know something about Candy and the boys."

***

"What's all the hullabaloo," Marshal Caine yelled out from the back side of the Yuma Jail. He had two drunks locked up and was looking forward to a supper with Linda Chavez. "Sounds like every bell in the city is being rung."

"The fire bells and every church bell, Marshal. Looks like one hell of fire down on the riverfront." Deputy Marshal Jim Rodgers, standing on the porch, yelled back. "Got a stampede heading that way. Ain't seen a fire that big in a long time."

"I'll get down there, Jim. Something like this will always bring out the worst in people. Why don't you take a nice walk around the plaza and watch for people breaking into some of the stores? Don't take no guff, neither. Chances are, they'll draw down on you, so best to bring that double-barreled shotgun."

Caine made his way as best he could to the docks and stood in awe of the destruction. "My god," he said. The steamboat Yuma Queen was fully engulfed, and the fire had spread to the heavy timbers of the dock. Embers from the massive conflagration settled on roof after roof of warehouses lining the riverfront street.

"Every building on the waterfront will go," Caine muttered. He didn't have to imagine what the toll might be. With the big ships at dock it meant they had come in from Mexico filled with product and those warehouses hadn't had time to move much.

The city's masses were jammed along the boardwalks of Riverfront Drive, getting in the way, shoving others aside for a better view, some panicked, others taking the opportunity to reach in someone's pocket or purse. Fights broke out, knives flashed in the bright firelight and more than one gunshot was heard.

Caine had just two deputies, Jim Rodgers and old

man Gonzales, the night jail man, so there was no crowd control when disasters such as this happened. He broke up a couple of fights, helped get men on the pumper breaks, helped get injured out of the way and headed for some kind of treatment. The marshal found himself running out of energy and knew it was all but useless to even be on the scene.

The various fire companies drew water from the river and their large pumpers were spewing gushers onto the flames but losing battle after battle. Caine could see many injured, laid out, propped up and tended to by some of the town's women. Others were laid out and covered head to toe with canvas.

Evening breezes were following the river and blowing flaming embers high into the desert sky and Caine could watch them descend, still hot, still burning, onto roof tops. *My god, if these winds continue this fire will wipe out all of Yuma. The fire boys will never be able to stop it. I've got to get back to town and spread the alarm. I wonder how involved Chastain is in this?*

Deputy Marshal Jim Rodgers was making his way slowly along the boardwalks of the central plaza when he saw two men about to break out the windows of a gun shop. "Good way to go to hell fast, boys. Best move it along and if I see you anywhere near the plaza tonight, I'll shoot you on sight."

There was no hesitation and Jim had to chuckle, watching them hightail it toward the river. Then he heard two distinct gunshots. "Sounds like they came from Johnny Simon's place," he muttered. He sped across the wide plaza and around the central fountain and saw several men sprinting from the Wagon Works.

"Johnny, you in there?" Rodgers yelled again. "You there?"

"We're here, Jim. Come on in," Johnny said. "Chased off some thievin' bastards. I know I'm not supposed to be shooting in town and I didn't shoot right at 'em but should have."

"Think I would have," Rodgers laughed. "What's this?" He was pointing at the wounded and dead on the floor.

"Chastain's men. Marshal Candy along with Snake and Dog-man are chasing Chastain now. He tried to burn out and kill the Otter family." Johnny said. "It looks like that fire is getting worse, Jim. Where's Marshal Caine?"

"Who the hell's Marshal Candy? Only man named Candy I know of is the barman on the docks."

"That's him," Johnny laughed. "He's a U.S. Deputy Marshal. We've been on the chase all day and thought we had Chastain, but he was able to get away. It's a mess, Jim. Sure could use Caine's help."

"Was old Buck Gabbard involved? Interesting that we haven't seen him all day."

"Involved to the point of being held in restraints as we speak at the Otter place. Chastain brought the fine sheriff and three deputies to burn out and kill the Otters. Chastain has to be here in town someplace."

"Hidden away in stacks of gold coins at the Bordertown Saloon, more than likely," Rodgers said. "Caine was headed down to the fire. I'll try to find him. Those hot cinders are falling everywhere." He turned toward the big doors just as Candy, Dog-man, and Snake came running in.

"Johnny, glad you're safe," Snake said. "Hated

to leave you like we did. These the left-overs?" He nudged the man with the broken legs. "Lost Chastain in all the mess along the river." Snake turned and saw Jim Rodgers, his badge shining in the firelight. "So, you work for Caine or Gabbard?"

"He works for me," Brod Caine said. "Just what the hell is going on, anyway. Fire's gonna take out the town, Jim. Gotta spread the word." Caine was breathing hard from the climb back to the plaza. "The Yuma Queen is lost along with half a dozen warehouses and now the wind has come up."

"Anybody die in that fire?" Snake didn't want to hear the answer but had to ask the question.

"It appears so," Caine said. "Lots of injured down there, too."

Marshal Caine looked around, spotted wounded and dead on the floor of the Wagon Works, then spotted George Candy. "Just what the hell is going on. What are you doing here?"

"We haven't been properly introduced, Marshal. I'm Deputy U.S. Marshal George Candy. I've been ordered to investigate and arrest Millard Chastain. We have a lot to talk about, Marshal and not a lot of time to do it."

"The wind's changing," Shorty yelled out. He was standing at the big doors with his shotgun, watching the crowds, the fire, and most of all, the embers floating toward tinder dry roofs and overhangs. "Blowing the fire back into the river."

"Let's hope it stays that way. Is Pedro open? We need to sit down with food and drink and figure out how to put all this together." Shorty nodded and the group walked out of the wagon shop leaving the wounded and dead but closing the big doors.

27

Chastain was hustled away from the waterfront by three of the boatmen and was in his gambling parlor and saloon in minutes. "I've got to get to Mexico, boys. That barman Candy is a U.S. Marshal and he's after me hard. Gotta get money and papers put together and get to Mexico. There's money for all that help."

"Where's Gabbard? He knows all the roads south." One of the burly boatmen said.

"Probably dead by now," Chastain muttered. He drank down half a glass of whiskey and was getting his big safe open. "You men, gather some horses, get up a crew to ride with me and put some guards outside the saloon with orders to shoot to kill." Jimmy Prescott led the other two, Boyd Cramer and a man call Cinch, out of the office.

After the men left Chastain went back to pulling stacks of money out of the safe and shoving them in canvas bags. He had bundled cash and racks of gold and silver coins, as used in banks and counting houses.

Spike Tamblin walked in, filthy dirty, covered in soot and dried blood. "Where the hell have you been?" Chastain stopped shoveling money into sacks and just stared at Tamblin. Sonny, Spike's son, followed, equally covered in grime and soot.

"That man Candy ain't no barkeep, Chastain. He's a federal marshal. Left us tied up at that bar of his. Couple of guys came in to steal whiskey when the fire broke out and saved our hides." Tamblin was mean, ready to kill at a moment's notice, but also had a quick mind.

"Looks like someone's planning to run off, Sonny. Might not be a bad idea if we joined him, eh?"

"Since he has the money." Sonny laughed. "Where we heading, Mil?"

"You help get me to Mexico, you'll be paid well. Candy don't want to take me in, he wants to kill me and I'll pay for protection. Can't take one of the boats. Got men gathering horses now."

Chastain was speaking fast, as a frightened man will do. He had more than a lifetime's money to protect and had assets in Mexico where he would be safe. He didn't own the steamboats, but he ran the gambling on them and had two gambling halls in Guaymas. He controlled the gambling along the waterfront in that Mexican deep port.

Shipping from around the world stopped in Guaymas, deep water commercial fishing was excellent, and the seaport was busy around the calendar. "Get me to Guaymas and I'll not only pay you well, I'll also have employment for you." Chastain showed just how desperate he was, letting these men see how much money he had right there in front of them.

Spike Tamblin found himself staring at the bags

of cash and looked instead at the little peacock of a gambler. He was trying his best to estimate how much cash each of those bags might hold and quit when the numbers exceeded his ability to count. "Sonny and me will give you as much protection as we can, Mil. I've always been your man."

"That you have," Chastain said. He saw the greed in the man's eyes as he watched the transfer of cash to bag. "We'll leave as soon as the horses get here. Go get cleaned up, you look like hell."

It wouldn't be a long run to the Mexican border, but it would be long and difficult to make it all the way to Guaymas. Sonny Tamblin had been working on the steamboats, knew how far it was, and knew that he and his father would have Chastain's canvas bags full before they reached the border. "Hope your boys are smart enough to bring a couple of pack animals, Mil. It's a long way to Guaymas."

"I figure we'll stop at farms on the way and get animals and food. Right now, I gotta get out of town. We gotta get moving."

Spike walked to the desk and hefted three of the canvas bags, nodded to Sonny to do the same, and headed for the door. Chastain grabbed up one, about all he could handle and followed. "Horse ain't gonna carry a man and these bags, Millard. Not for long, he won't." They stood just inside the doors of the gambling hall and watched for Chastain's men to show up with the animals.

Those along the bar and at the tables couldn't take their eyes off the large bags, they knew they must be filled with gold and cash and more than one began planning. Where would this little peacock be going? How many men would be riding with him? Did he start that fire? Three men rode up to the front of the saloon trailing four horses, saddled and bridled.

"All we could find, Mil. People are leaving town. Looks like the fire is coming this way." Jimmy Prescott stepped down. "Roads out of town are packed. It'll be a panic soon."

"Good," Chastain said. "Spike, go get my horse and get a couple for you and Sonny. Jimmy, help me get these bags tied off on two of those horses. We'll take Riverfront South and stop at a ranch for supplies. We'll be on a long road, boys."

Prescott was amazed at the weight of the canvas bags. There were seven of them and he distributed two to a horse with the extra one strapped behind his own saddle. Chastain was quick to notice that and said to change that to his horse. Chastain knew that Spike and Sonny would be thinking of ripping these bags from him but didn't expect it from Prescott.

"There's a lot of money and a position in my operation in Guaymas for those that protect and get me there. Lots of money, Jimmy. Can I count on you?" He knew he couldn't but maybe pitting Prescott against Spike would help. The others with the horses were Boyd Cramer, a born thief and a man simply known as Cinch.

Cinch came on the scene about six months ago, Chastain remembered, coming to Yuma from the San Francisco waterfront, he said. "You up to a ride like this, Cinch?"

"Rather be on a boat, Mr. Chastain," he said. "But I'll do what you need to be done. Sailed into Guaymas on a boat to Panama a couple of times.

Been to sea most of my life but I can ride a horse and shoot a man."

"That's what I want." Chastain took the reins from Spike when he brought the horses out front. Cinch lashed the last bag to the back of Chastain's horse and the gambler stepped into the saddle. He took the lead ropes of the three horses and led the group off toward the south road, most of Yuma, on the move, were heading east or north.

***

"See that?" Shorty Gunderson pointed out the window. "Isn't that Jimmy Prescott and Cinch riding in? They are Chastain's men. I don't know that other one."

"That's Boyd Cramer, Shorty. He's a thief and would shoot you in the back just for fun," Caine said. "Looks like they have some saddled horses with them. Most interesting."

Johnny Simon, Shorty, Candy and the rest were sitting at tables near the window of Pedro's, eating platters of enchiladas and bowls of beans. "You sure that's Cinch?" Candy asked. He didn't have a good look from where he was sitting. Man's been on my list for some time. Think I'll take a little walk."

"Want company?" Snake started to get up.

"No, I'll be right back." He slipped out the door and tried to keep in the deep shadows of the plaza, following Prescott and Cinch. He stood between two buildings about a hundred feet from where Chastain and the gang were loading large bags onto horses. Candy wanted to race back and bring Caine and rest but knew it would be much better to just know where this bunch would be riding.

Can't take on that whole bunch all by myself and sure as hell if I run back for help, they'll be gone before we get back. All our horses are still at the Wagon Works, too. Damn it. Have to know which way they're going.

It seemed the fire was being contained on the riverfront and the docks, but fire was the most frightening thing to most and Candy watched hordes of people leaving town. "Can't let them get lost in the crowd," he muttered. He moved slowly, staying in the shadows, to the next building so he could follow when they left.

He watched Chastain lead them out of the plaza and turn toward the south road. "Taking the river road," he muttered. He was almost running as he crossed the large plaza and made his way to Pedro's. "Chastain's heading south, has several men with him and pack horses carrying large sacks. My guess, they are filled with cash and gold. He'll be in Mexico quick and I'll lose him."

It was a foot race back to the Wagon Works and horses. "Hate to leave the feller with the broken leg but no time to find a doc now." Candy, Snake, Dog-man, and Caine had their horses saddled and waiting for them. "Catch up, Johnny and Shorty. We'll need your guns." Candy yelled out, spurring his horse out of the big building. "Take the south road and keep your eyes open."

Once they cleared the central area of Yuma it was easier going. Most of those fleeing the fire went north or east. The wind was following the river and they could see flames from the massive warehouses along the riverfront streaming hundreds of feet into the night air. "It looked like Chastain was leading several pack animals, so they won't be moving fast. Let's not ride into a trap," Candy said.

The roadway wasn't heavily used and followed terrain along the river, threading its way around stands of cactus, rocks, and the rises and falls of the land. The land was sparse, undulating enough to hamper distant views and the air was filled with acrid smoke from burning docks, boats, and warehouses. The dark night sky was shrouded in smoke, hiding the bright stars that might have put some distinction to the trail.

"There are a few farms down this way, poor people scratching out a miserable life in this sandy hell," Shorty Gunderson said. "They're a pretty protective bunch. What did you say Chastain had on those pack animals?"

"Canvas sacks, Shorty. I doubt if they're filled with food and water," Candy said. Guffaws and chuckles filled the air for a few moments along with a snort or two. "Most likely cash and gold. Chastain is a good, if cheating gambler, but he's making the wrong bet here. He won't live to see the border with the men he's riding with. They'll kill him then fight among themselves for the prize."

Snake looked over at Dog-man and gave him a sad smile. "We got no business being here, Dog. We should be with April and those kids. I was wrong. Let's wrap this up and ride back to Tucson, make sure April is really fine, and then ride straight for San Diego."

"You really are a good man, Snake, but you're right, too. We do have a fight with this Chastain feller. He was gonna kill the Otter family.

I know you can't abide something like that."

"Maybe we can stop at their place on the way back, Dog. I don't want a wife, Dog. I don't want to be living in the same place days on end. I'm thinking of what Caine said about people dying when we set that boat afire. What we did ain't right. What we did for the Otters, that was right. What we did for April, that was right. And those wonderful little brats. I miss them."

"We'll get it all figured out after we get Millard Chastain in irons and in Candy's custody, Snake." Dog-man said. "Lot's of time to talk, then."

"Why do I have these feelings for the kids? That's what I want. A whole passel of kids."

Dog-man was laughing hard enough to catch everyone's attention and tried to slough it off. "Snake's being a comedian, is all." The vision of Snake leading a string of kids, all horseback and carrying lariats was more than he could hold in. "Damn, Snake, I'd really like to see that."

"Can't have it, though. Mr. Potter got tied up with the wrong woman but came out of it with a couple of kids. Sure wouldn't want to be like him. My mind is so messed up, Dog. Let's get this Chastain fool and get the hell out of here."

Dog-man knew he had nothing to add, nothing Snake would want to hear, anyway and nudged his horse into a little faster walk. *That's one complicated Texas drover right there. If there's a pretty girl in trouble, he'll help, but if there are children involved, nothing will stop him.*

"Ranch to the left, boys," Marshal Caine said. "Should be the Hernandez place. Hector Hernandez and Rosa. They've got some of the meanest dogs in the territory." There were dim lights far off the road and Snake turned his attention to the road they were on.

"See any fresh tracks, Caine? We've been just riding and should have been paying attention. Anyone turning into that ranch?" Snake was growling, trying to get what Dog-man said out of his mind.

"Hard to tell in the dark like this," Caine said.

"I'm afraid you're a city boy, Marshal." Dog-man rode up to the head of the group. "Hold back some," he said. He rode out in front and gave the roadway a good going over. "Lots of horses in a group and recent," he muttered. He rode right up to the lane leading to the Hernandez place. He could hear a pack of dogs letting Hernandez know they were there.

"Went right on by," he said. "I'll take point for a while if you don't mind, Marshal." Sparse vegetation, deep sand, and open desert lay in front and Dog-man stayed on the roadway. Following a trail as broad as Chastain was leaving, wasn't difficult and they picked up the pace. The river was taking some sharp turns, others broad and wide, but the road was straighter.

"We should see another ranch in the next half hour," Caine said. "Gabilan family. Jorge Gabilan, married to an Indian, three teen-age daughters. They do the work, Jorge drinks."

28

"Should have stopped at that first place, Mr. Chastain. We need water. The animals need water." Cinch knew this country well and told Chastain it would be at least another thirty miles if they didn't stop now. "There is no water in this open desert."

"All right, Cinch, lead us in. Whose place is this?"

"Never heard names. Mexican man, Indian wife, and three daughters. Lazy bastard, but a productive little farm. Should be able to get food and water for several days. We'll need to make several stops like this along the way. We're many days from Guaymas."

Spike and Sonny slowed their horses down just a bit until they were slightly separated from the group. "This will be our opportunity, Sonny. Jimmy will go with whatever we do. Don't know about Cinch or Boyd. When we know how much food is available, we can gun Chastain down, take out the family and make a run for the border."

That was it for planning, but father and son lived wild and free their entire lives and planning had little to do with how they managed. "We ain't goin' to Guaymas, though, are we?" Sonny asked.

"Hell no, boy. Ride east and then north. Getting into Mexico first will head off whatever law wants to follow us." The border was flexible in many places, but treaties were not and lawmen on both sides abided by them. Spike lived many years along the border and understood that.

Cinch led the group down the long lane to an adobe farmhouse. Dim light could be seen from the inset windows and dogs started barking not long after they made the turn. "They know we're coming, boys," Chastain said. "Let's be friendly until we know how many guns they have."

Six men with a four-horse pack train rode right up to the little house and Jimmy Prescott yelled out, "Hello the house. We come in peace."

Gabilan opened the door, spreading light across the riders. "It's late. What do you want?" He wasn't wearing a firearm and Cinch thought it unusual to open the door and not be carrying something, shotgun, rifle, pitchfork. Gabilan stood just above five feet, rotund, and wore a bushy mustache. What little hair he had left hung loose well below his shoulders.

"We need water for the animals," Chastain said. "Where is your well?" The gambler broke one of the few laws of the frontier and stepped down from his horse before being invited. "Need food for the trail, too." He walked right up to the heavy farmer and pushed him back inside the house, followed by Prescott and Spike Tamblin.

"Take care of the animals, Cinch," Sonny Tamblin said. "I'll see what kind of food I can find. Need meat and beans, coffee and flour, for sure. I thought Chastain said to ride in friendly?"

Cinch chuckled. "That's as friendly as he gets. Looks like salt barrels over there. Hope they're filled with meat." He walked all the animals to a round, open rock trough and let them have their fill. "We're about five miles from the border and we won't find many more ranches for a couple of days, Sonny."

"Ain't much worried about that," Sonny said and then quickly shut up. *Damn. Didn't mean to say that. Hope Cinch ain't too bright. Damn. Spike'll kill me if he finds out.* "Good brined meat in these barrels but sure can't carry them. Gotta go in and talk to Spike."

"I'll be right in," Cinch said. He waited until Sonny closed the door behind him and sprinted out to where the farm lane turned off from the highway and tied a kerchief to a post, then hustled back to the farmyard and into the little house.

Chastain had the Gabilan family seated around their table in the kitchen, except for the heavy Indian woman, Gabilan's wife. She was making coffee. Three young girls, from twelve or so to sixteen, were seated with their father. Cinch noted that not one in the Gabilan family stood taller than five-feet-three inches and all were more than stout.

Spike and Jimmy were eyeing the oldest of the girls but it was Boyd Cramer who had eyes on Mrs. Gabilan. *Gonna be a lot of trouble around here and soon.* Cinch got himself in a position that would be fairly safe when gunfire began. He watched Sonny and Spike move for good shots at Chastain and some protection from Boyd and himself. Prescott stood off almost as an observer.

"There are barrels of brined meat, Chastain, but no way to pack it. We'd need a wagon to haul them along with water." Sonny Tamblin said. "This road doesn't really go anywhere once we're across the border. We've moved several miles inland from the river and it's just south of the border where the river empties into the gulf."

"There are villages along the coast. We'll be fine," Chastain said. "Fishing villages along the coast, ranches too." Chastain got up and stood next to Gabilan. "Have your woman wrap up enough meat for four days."

"No comprende, señor," Gabilan said, bringing a snicker to Cinch and Jimmy Prescott. The Tamblins glared at them.

"You speak English," Chastain roared. "I heard you. Now, get your woman making packs of meat." He reached across the table and yanked the eldest daughter to her feet. "Make up packs of flour, coffee and sugar. Now, girl," he yelled, shoving her toward her mother.

Gabilan spoke briefly to his wife, in Spanish and she and the girl left the room. Cinch kept a straight face hearing the old man tell the girl to ride for help. He watched helplessly as Spike turned, pulled his revolver and shot Millard Chastain in the knee. Chastain fell to the floor, crying out in pain.

"Once more for good luck," Spike said. He shot him in the other knee, laughing loud and then shot him in one of his feet. "Good luck on your excursion south, Mil."

Sonny had his pistol out and aimed in the general direction of Boyd Cramer and Jimmy Prescott. "With us or not?" He said softly. Neither man moved but both nodded their heads slightly. He turned to Cinch who also nodded.

The two young girls were screaming in terror seeing Chastain's blood splashed around their kitchen, Jorge Gabilan was frozen in fear not able to move and Spike shoved him back to his seat. "That's settled." He looked at Gabilan. "You have a wagon?"

"Small cart. One donkey. That is all," Gabilan said.

"I better check on that woman," Boyd Cramer said. "She's been gone too long."

Spike smiled, knowing Cramer didn't give a damn how long the woman had been gone, just wanted to be with her. Cramer slipped out the kitchen door and when Gabilan made a move to follow, Spike shot him dead. The two young girls screamed and rushed to their father's body. "Get them out of here," Spike growled.

Cinch moved the girls into another room and told them to be quiet or they would be next. He held his hand on his sidearm as he spoke and the message was loud and clear. When he returned to the kitchen, he found Prescott going through Chastain's pockets. "Get yours while you can, eh?" He said. "Does Spike have any more of a plan than Chastain had? Simply crossing the border ain't gonna get us anywhere and sure as hell somebody's gonna be lookin'."

"I'm gonna get what I can and get the hell back to Tucson, then Santa Fe. You'd be smart to do the same, Cinch. Spike and Sonny are gonna kill Cramer as soon as he's through with the old lady, then come looking for us."

"Figured as much. Think I'll check on what's going on outside." Cinch was careful to move slowly toward the door, watching Prescott the whole way. Chastain was bleeding, whimpering in pain, but nobody paid him the least attention.

There was no reason to kill that old man, and the woman is next. Prescott doesn't have a clue and neither does Cramer. Spike and Sonny are going to kill everyone here, but how are they going to get all that money out of here? They can't stay long below the border without food and water. Cinch knew he didn't have the kind of plan Spike might want.

***

Gabilan's wife led her daughter to the horses and untied one, getting the girl in the saddle. "Ride to the Hernandez ranch and bring help. Hurry, Rosita, hurry. Those men are killers." Rosita was gone in seconds and Gabilan's wife was at the brine barrels when a single gunshot rang out. She knew instantly that it was Jorge who died.

Jorge spent most of every day drinking tequila and sleeping, letting his wife and daughters tend to the farm. He called his wife Mamacita because he couldn't pronounce her Indian name which translated to something about white clouds and wind. She ran to the small shed where they kept the two-wheeled cart, but also kept the shotgun and shells.

She had just reached for the door to the shed when Boyd Cramer grabbed her. He had her inside the shed and on the ground in an instant, trying to both lift her skirts and get his pants down. She was a fighter, and kicked him in the groin and when he rolled over, she was on her feet racing for the back of the shed.

It's a proven fact that a woman can run with her skirts in hand faster than a man with his pants around his knees and Mamacita reached her shotgun well before Boyd Cramer reached her. She pulled the triggers just as fast as she could and saw Cramer flung backward, spewing blood everywhere.

She was quick getting the big gun reloaded and knew where the donkey was, even in the dark and led him out of the shack, mounting after clearing the door. "That's far enough, woman," Spike Tamblin said. She slid back off the animal.

29

Rosita wasn't a good rider but put the horse in as good a lope as she could manage and rode for the Hernandez ranch in a pitch-black night. If she stayed on the road it would take her there but she wished there was a bright moon or more stars. Not aware of the fire in nearby Yuma of course, she didn't understand the heavy smoke. The five riders seemed to come at her from out of nowhere.

"Easy, girl, we're not going to hurt you." Shorty had the reins and brought the horse to a stop. "You're Jorge Gabilan's daughter, aren't you?"

"Yes, señor. There is trouble. I'm riding to the Hernandez ranch for help." Fear shone brightly in her eyes as she looked at the five big men covered in dust and ash. She had just watched men invade her home and now more had hold of her. "I must hurry, please," she cried.

"I'm Deputy Marshal Candy, Miss Gabilan. Nobody's going to hurt you. We're chasing outlaws and that might be why you're looking for help, eh?" The giant of a lawman overwhelmed the chubby little girl, but his soft voice and kind words worked their magic and she blurted out what happened at the farm.

"We must hurry. They will kill mama and papa. They are going to take all our food. I'm scared," she wailed. Snake rode up to her side in an instant. He lifted her from the saddle and had her in his arms, talking softly, rubbing her shoulders, even speaking what he called Mexi-can, a mix of Texas brush country and Spanish.

It took just seconds and she quieted down, stopped crying, but held tight onto Snake. "They're all going to die," she whimpered.

"Rosita, we must hurry," Snake said.

"Let's make dust, gentlemen." Candy put the spurs to his horse and Snake kept the girl with him and led her horse as they rode hard for the Gabilan farm. They pulled up at the entrance to the lane. "My goodness sakes," Candy said. He pulled a rag from a post and held it up. "We have some help, boys and I'm thinking he needs our help, too."

Snake eased the girl back onto her horse. "You stay here until one of us comes to get you," he said. "It's going to be very dangerous at the house. We'll find your mama and papa and get them safe as quickly as we can."

"What kind of help?" Dog-man asked. Caine and Johnny grunted their question as well.

"This rag belongs to Deputy U.S. Marshal Brady Cinch. He's become one of Chastain's gang members, feeding me information," Candy said. "This tells me they are all at this farm. He must have spotted me when they rode out of Yuma. Let's give him some help."

"How far from here to the farmhouse?" Snake asked the girl. She told him and he stepped down from the saddle. "Best if we go in on foot, boys. Want to make this a surprise party if we can."

***

"Where do you think you're goin'?" Spike had his gun out and aimed in the general direction of Mamacita Gabilan. You plannin' to run off? Maybe we'll just change your plans." He never saw the shotgun, held vertically and in the folds of her dress and when he took a step toward her, she pulled it up to blow him in half.

It must have been in his good-luck stars for the barrel caught in Mamacita's skirts and the two barrels fired their loads of death into the dirt at Spike's feet. Some of the pellets went through his boots and a few just a bit higher and Tamblin fell to the ground, crying out in pain. Anger flushed through his body. "You witch," he screamed and despite the pain, he emptied his revolver into the large woman.

"You miserable witch," he bellowed again. He was trying to get to his feet when Sonny and Cinch came running up. Prescott just ambled over a sneer obvious when he looked at Spike's bleeding legs.

"Boyd's dead," Prescott said.

Cinch caught a movement behind Spike and eased off to the side looking around to find out where Sonny was. He spotted him coming out of the shed and moved to intercept him. *Don't know how many men Candy has but that had to be him I saw. Chastain's hurt bad and Boyd is dead, Spike's hurt, so I need to take out Sonny right now.*

He raised the rifle and aimed it at Sonny Tamblin. "Stop right there, Sonny. Let's ease that smoker to the ground, eh? Nice and easy, boy. Chastain and Spike are wounded, Boyd's dead and you're on your way to prison. Drop it, now. Oh, by the way, I'm Deputy U.S. Marshal Cinch."

He spoke loud hoping that Candy would hear and got his answer immediately. "This is Marshal Candy and a large posse. One move and you all die. Drop your weapons and sit down. I won't say it again."

Sonny hesitated but only for a moment when he saw men coming at him with rifles and shotguns. He eased his sidearm out and dropped it on the ground. "Kick it over here, Sonny," Cinch said. "Sit down," he commanded.

Jimmy Prescott stood quietly in the shadows looking in every direction for an escape avenue and slowly eased himself toward the farmhouse door. It was late at night and he was hidden in the dark. Inside he moved to the room where the two Gabilan daughters were on the floor sobbing. "On your feet," he said. "Up, girl." He grabbed one by her long hair and jerked her to her feet. The other got up fast.

"I'll hurt you bad if you scream or try to run," he said. He jerked the girl's hair again to make his point. "You stay in front of me," he said and was going to move back out to where the horses were. He stopped and ripped a long strip from one of the girl's dresses and tied their arms behind them and tied them together at the necks. He held the end of the rag and marched them out of the farmhouse. They could hear moans coming from Chastain as they passed.

"You men move away from those horses." Prescott yelled out. He had the rag end in one hand

and his revolver in the other as he moved slowly toward his horse, tied near the rock trough. "Back away and these girls will live, make one wrong move and they die. All I want is a horse and five minutes to ride out."

Dog-man had gone into the shed to check on Boyd's body and stood in the shadows watching. He moved to the back of the shed where the donkey had been and eased out the doors there.

"Can't do that, Jimmy," Marshal Candy said. "Spike just told me Chastain's dead. It's over, Jimmy. There ain't nothin' left to take. Let the girl's go. You'll do some hard time but that's better than dyin'. Let go of the girls, Jimmy."

"Chastain ain't dead, Marshal. Just shot up some. Now, move back or these girls will die, one at a time. Back now."

Prescott was a small-time thief, gambler with marked decks, not a great thinker and all he could see was that canvas sack tied to the back of his horse. It would be a whole new life with fine and clean clothes, lovely women and good food. He saw four big guns aimed at him but had these girls. His safety, his getaway, his freedom was those girls.

"No," he said. "Back away or these girls die, one at a time. I want my horse and five minutes."

The rifle butt crushed the back of his head and he lurched forward, dropping his gun and the rag tied to the girls. "Damn fool," Dog-man said. He quickly gathered up the girls and got them untied. Snake was there in an instant, hustling them away from Prescott's body and near the shed.

Shorty made the quick run to the road and brought Rosita, the eldest Gabilan daughter into the farmyard. "We've got a mess, Johnny," he said. "So much death. So much sorrow. What happens to these children, this farm?"

Johnny Simon was sitting on his haunches, drawing lines in the dirt with a twig, staring at nothing. "All for some gold," he murmured.

30

Smoke was still in the air as the sun came up. Bodies were laid out, covered in what was available. Rosita, almost sixteen-years-old rode off to the Hernandez ranch to ask if someone could ride for a priest and Candy had the Tamblin men dig graves. They pulled shotgun pellets from Spike's legs and feet but wouldn't listen to his complaints.

Cinch had Millard Chastain laid out in the dirt by a fire, working to clean the wounds to his knees and foot. "Gonna be hard time at Huntsville for you, Chastain. Gonna be even harder, you bein' a cripple and all. Sure hope that Sheriff Gabbard lived. He'll be a fine witness against you and the many you've destroyed, too."

"Those people who died at the Yuma Queen fire have to be answered for," Candy said.

Chastain never said a word, just whimpered from the pain. Was some of that crying related to the fact he would never walk again? Did he even understand what life in a miserable federal prison might be like for a man who couldn't walk? All the bravado, swagger, arrogance was gone, replaced by whimpering and crying out in pain.

Snake sat at the trough with the younger girls as they had their breakfast. The house was nowhere to be this morning. "Yes, Marshal Candy, those who died at the fire need to be answered for. Are you sure what we did is justified? Dog-man and I participated fully but were we right. Did those innocent people have to die?" Snake had been almost in pain listening to himself ask those questions all night long.

"Chastain is the man responsible for everything that has happened," Candy said. "Everything we've done is justified. Chastain has killed innocent people, ruined lives, destroyed families and hurt people by the score, Snake. His capture and what we did to accomplish this, is fully justified." Candy and Cinch walked off to have a discussion about how to transport their prisoners back to Yuma.

Snake wasn't ready to accept Candy's decision on justified death, looked almost with pleading eyes to Dog-man. "What do we do with these girls, Dog? They can't stay here. Rosita isn't old enough to run this farm and raise these girls."

"I'll bet you she is," Dog-man said. He sat down on the rough rocks of the trough with a plate full of side meat and gravy. "She's one tough little cookie, Snake. Kinda like another little girl we know."

"I've had little Geneva on my mind all morning, Dog. Her and her brothers, her mama. I don't care what Marshal Candy just said, we were wrong burning that boat. You're gonna think I'm crazy but when we get this mess we've got ourselves in all cleaned up, I want to ride back to Tucson and make sure April is going to make it. That man from the sale yard seemed right at the time, but I want to be sure."

"You're not gonna like it if you find out April married him." Dog-man poured some coffee for the two of them. "You're a deep man, Snake. Too deep to be a drifter. It was our idea to burn Chastain out, not Candy's. That's what's bothering you, isn't it? We have more money than we can count in our accounts, maybe you should quit being afraid of settled life."

"I'll ponder on both those thoughts on our ride back to Tucson. Right now, I've got these little girls. I'll have a talk with Rosita when she gets back. Marshal Candy and Marshal Caine can worry about prisoners and bodies, I've got these girls to worry about."

Dog-man had to smile as he finished his meal and walked off to see Johnny Simon and Shorty Gunderson. "Looks like your cousin Virginia's problems with Millard Chastain are over, Johnny. What are your plans?"

"Shorty and I are riding back to Yuma shortly. See how much of the old town is left. Caine's riding with us. You and Snake are surely welcome."

"Snake has to make sure the Gabilan girls are going to be okay, then we will. He'll make sure we stop at Otter's place, too, on the way out. He has families all over the territory," Dog-man laughed.

"He's as good a friend as anyone could ask for," Johnny said. "Looks like Rosita's coming back. Hope she could get a priest. It's important for these people."

Rosita jumped off her horse and ran to Snake, throwing her arms around the rangy Texan. "We will have a priest for Mama and Papa," she cried out.

"He is on his way." She kissed Snake on the cheek and ran to her sisters. "Come, girls. We have a house to clean. These men have made a mess of our home. Come along, now."

Snake smiled, kicked sone dust. "They'll be fine," he murmured. "I think we need to get back to Yuma, Dog, see if the old town survived. I don't think they need us around here anymore." Dog-man looked at Johnny Simon as if to say, "See, I told you so."

The ride back to Yuma in daylight was much easier, strong breezes blew much of the smoke away, but as they got closer to town it was obvious the fire had caused considerable damage.

"Marshal Candy said whatever damage the fire caused was going to be charged to Chastain," Dog-man said. "Looks to me that those canvas bags are gonna be empty soon." The fire moved up from the riverfront and devastated the first two blocks before being stopped when the wind changed. Simon's Wagon Works, right in the central plaza was saved as was the Bordertown saloon and Pedro's Cantina.

"Wonder where Buck Gabbard is?" Snake reined his horse up in front of the wagon shop. "We just left him there with Jeremiah Otter."

"I'm wondering if the dead and injured are still tied up inside here," Dog-man said. "We just rode off, not even blowin' 'em a kiss." He stepped down and walked toward the big doors.

"Caine will probably be called on to be both city marshal and county sheriff," Johnny said. "Chastain's days of running things are over, but the criminal element that he produced will still be active. Bet he asks you two to stick around for a while."

"Bet we say no," Snake laughed. "I'm gonna go

over there to Pedro's, eat half a dozen enchiladas, drink half a keg of cold beer and sleep the rest of the day away in one of your empty stalls. Tomorrow will tell a different story, and I'm sure it will deal with Candy, Caine, Cinch, and Gabbard, but not today."

***

"Let's whoa up, Dog. Gotta talk." It was about five miles from Yuma to the Otter farm and they were only about half-way. Snake walked his horse several hundred feet off the road and tied it off to some thorny brush. "Need a small fire and some coffee, old man."

"You worrying up a problem?" Dog-man helped get the fire going and put together a quick pot of coffee. For many this might seem strange, but for Dog-man it was Snake's way. Snake would spend hours thinking out problems and reaching conclusions, finally needing to get them out in the open. "Hope it's a friendly problem this time."

"This is what we do best, Dog. Sit on the ground near a good fire, free as the wind whistling through the brambles. But we've always had a plan, loose as all get out sometimes, but a plan. We had a plan until we got to Yuma."

"That bothers you, doesn't it?" Dog-man stirred the fire and added a few twigs to keep the pot hot. "California, Snake. Ever since we left Las Cruces, that's been our plan. I don't want to see much more of Arizona Territory. We did right by April and her children, but when we got mixed up in this Chastain business, it ain't been right."

"That's exactly right. We got no reason to ride out and check on the Otter family. Only reason we even know them is their barn burned. They got neat kids and I'll think about 'em often, like I will Geneva, but what's important right now, Dog, is us making up a real plan again."

"San Diego was the original plan when we left Las Cruces. Got us all side-tracked, Snake. We heard about them damned steamboats and got us all messed up. Well, we seen 'em."

Snake was laughing hard enough to spill his coffee. "Seen one, burned it down and put its owner out of business. Job's done, Dog. It's San Diego for us."

"We'll ride back and fill our packs out proper, take the ferry across that muddy river, and make our way. I'd really like to see this fine country they call California. I think it was Puny Russell told about that big wide valley runs up the middle of California. Said if you dropped a seed it would knock you down growin' so fast."

"You still thinking of a ranch, ain't you? I'm ready for several days on the trail, alone with the wind and the stars, Dog." They knocked the fire down and tuned back for Yuma. "Don't want to hear about nobody gettin' in trouble."

***

"We know this is a good trail on to the coast, but what exactly will we be looking at?" Snake and Dogman were talking with the old man at the trading center in Yuma. They were filling out their packs for the almost two-hundred-mile ride.

"Not much of nothing. A long dry ride, boys.

There's a soft valley in a hundred miles, but ain't no real towns or villages. Here's a good map with water holes located. Not much Indian trouble, some banditos up from the border and not much game, either. Take dried meat, lots of beans, flour and sugar. Don't forget the coffee."

"Somewhere along the way we have misplaced our pack animal and need to put that on the shopping list, too," Dog-man said.

They were standing on the high wooden dock of the trading post looking west. "The other side of that big old muddy river is California, Dog-man. We'll take one of the ferries across and be free as the wind. Got two good mules this time, old man." Snake's eyes were shining, and Dog-man gave him a good look over.

He was right. He would have loved April, held her closer, but this day would arrive. This day when the pack mule is loaded, when the road beckons. He'll always love her and her children, but no woman could ever replace that long empty road out there. "Let's ride, Pard."

The ferryman charged them five dollars to take the two horses, two pack mules and two men across the river. "Closest we're gonna get to taking a long trip on this waterway, Dog."

"Ever since that feller back in Gila Bend talked about steamboats, I wanted to go on a trip on one. Instead, old friend, we burned one to the water line. Guess we'll have to settle for this fine craft."

They stepped off the ferry and walked up a little incline to the top of the river's bank. "We're here," Snake said. "This is California. Didn't think we'd ever really get here. What's on your mind?"

"Don't look much different that where we were," Dog-man said. "No need to rush. Should be in San Diego in ten days or so unless you spot a burnin' barn or something." He didn't get any response and nudged his horse into a walk.

The road followed just north of the border with Mexico, probably dipped and turned into Mexico from time to time, but with well plotted water holes, the boys were off just as the sun peaked its head over the Gila Mountains. "California, we are here," Dog-man muttered, giving his horse a little nudge with his spurs.

"You see any burning barns, keep it to yourself, Snake."

Snake grumbled for a moment then burst into laughter. "No burning barns, no steamships in the desert. Just us, Partner, making our way across a vast desert to San Diego. That's our next stop." Dog-man couldn't hold in his laughter seeing his partner stretched languidly across the back of his saddle.

"San Diego it is, and we don't have to be in any kind of hurry."

A Look at Name's Corcoran, Terrence Corcoran (Terrence Corcoran Book I)

Terrence Corcoran carried a badge in Virginia City, Nevada until one day, in a drunken stupor, he shot the sheriff. Now he's returning to the Comstock looking to get his badge back and stumbles into a conspiracy that might put the sheriff, district attorney, and others in jail for a long time. A lovely working girl is brutally murdered, a Hungarian duke wants a Wells Fargo gold shipment, and the sheriff rehires him after first kicking him in a most tender spot. Corcoran was born on the ship bringing his family to this country, ran away to the frontier at an early age and brings his ideas of the old country and knowledge learned of the west to whatever mess he finds himself in. He's carried a badge, found himself in jail, and stands four-square for right, honor, and truth. You gotta love the guy.

AVAILABLE NOW ON AMAZON